You Are Loved

Uh, oh.

Cassie was sure to walk out the door soon. It seemed to be in the town script.

Jake was surprised. His eyes dropped.

She sounded and looked angry. Really angry.

She must know who did it and was protecting her. Why else would she react so strongly?

Of course, once again, maybe she represented the thoughts of the whole town—they wanted it kept secret. Left alone. Maybe they all knew. After all, Holly sounded angry, too. Not to mention Kelly.

His head swirled with the one constant question he couldn't find an answer to.

Why was it kept quiet?

What was the big deal?

He didn't understand it.

This mystery woman had literally saved his life and now he found she helped others as well. Surely this woman should be applauded for all the good work she does. He longed to hear her story and why she rainbowed people. She deserved recognition and just maybe people would emulate her more and pass on her good intentions. This would definitely make the world a better place.

You Are Loved

Suzanne M. Hurley

A Wings ePress, Inc.
Inspirational Romance Novel

Edited by: Jeanne Smith
Copy Edited by: Bev Haynes
Executive Editor: Jeanne Smith
Cover Artist: Trisha FitzGerald-Jung
Image from Pixabay

Wings ePress Books
www.wingsepress.com

ISBN 978-1-61309-897-4

Published In the United States Of America

Wings ePress, Inc.
3000 N. Rock Road
Newton, KS 67114

Dedication

During the pandemic, I received the best gift ever—the deepening of my friendship with my neighbor, Helen Anderson. Helen just turned 100 years young, and I have benefited from her wisdom, humor, and kindness. I dedicate this book to Helen, who is always there to listen and help me sort out just what I'm trying to say. Thank you, Helen.

I also remember Dorothy Bodoin, one of the greatest people ever, who has passed away. Dorothy wrote the first review of my first book and we became the best of friends. We e-mailed each other almost every single day for sixteen years. Dorothy, I will never, ever forget you and your kindness, support, and humor. I hope you are surrounded with your collies as you rest in peace. Thank you, Dorothy.

I also remember my beautiful sweet cat, Panda, who is now running free with Rico and John, pain-free and filled with joy.

To Mary Lou, Sheila, Theresa, Marja, and Lynda.

To my family, in thanksgiving, for all of their support.

To Jeanne Smith—the best editor ever—who helps clarify my thoughts.

To Trisha Fitzgerald, who designed the cover and the entire Wings ePress staff for their dedication and hard work.

Thank you.

Prologue

I stared at the camper truck.

Was someone really living there?

In the winter? The freezing cold?

Sadness descended.

Tears escaped, drifting down my cheeks.

Glancing down at the large bag in my hand holding a pink basket filled with bread, peanut butter, fruit, and cookies, I wondered out loud, "Should I leave it?"

My voice sounded loud and shrill as it echoed throughout the parking lot.

Oh! Oh! Big mistake. I had to remember it was still dark, no traffic, and sound travels. I didn't want the driver to know I was here.

What if I had read the situation wrong?

Or was being foolish.

Interfering.

Would the driver be upset? Angry?

Nervous as anything, I started to pace. Back and forth, back and forth, my boots leaving footprints on the freshly fallen snow. Pawprints, too. My dog was beside me, step by step.

I am scared. What if the driver thinks I'm an intruder, a thief, someone out to hurt him? My imagination soared. What if he comes bursting out with a weapon? A knife. A gun.

Frozen with fear, I stopped. Stood still.

Should I take the chance?

Or just leave.

After all, I wasn't really sure of what I was witnessing.

I looked down at my dog sitting patiently at my feet. "What do you think?" I asked softly, this time for his ears only.

He wagged his tail, always agreeing with me and ready for a new adventure. He was all for it.

Frantically, I started going over the facts. Every day I walk the same route in the early morning hours. Some say I'm crazy to be out here this early when I don't need to, but it is my meditative time where I experience peace and quiet before busyness takes over.

A week ago, I'd noticed the camper parked in various lots around town. The last three nights, it was in this exact spot near a local restaurant. It was definitely the same one, for I had noted a large scratch on the passenger side, and there it was. I wasn't imagining it.

A few days ago, while driving through town, I even saw a man behind the wheel, but was too far away to get a good look. Besides, he turned down a side street and following him was not something I'd do. I was definitely not a stalker.

But did he need help?

Was he really all alone?

Did he not have any other place to live?

I didn't want to believe it, but feared it was true.

I'd come to the horrid conclusion someone might be living in it and whoever it was probably slept in the back at night.

Tragic and so close to Christmas.

Concerned, I had put together a basket of food that might help.

Maybe. Could be he didn't need anything.

But I had never delivered an anonymous package to a truck. Was there even protocol for that?

Or maybe in this situation it shouldn't be anonymous. Should I make an exception? Knock on the door? Talk to him? Actually see the state he was in?

Oh, stop all this silly meandering. Go on, do it. Get it over with.

I stared up at the sky just as a shooting star exploded. Simultaneously, dramatically. Suddenly my mother's words flashed before me. "Love is all about giving, and sometimes you just need to listen to your gut and help out where you see fit."

Mom was right.

My gut knew this driver was in trouble.

Deep in my heart, I connected with him.

He needed help, kindness, compassion. To know someone cared.

I was sure of it.

And he needed it stat.

Here goes.

Tossing my fears, I whispered to my dog, "Come."

I crept forward.

My dog followed and as we drew nearer, I turned my head back and forth, keeping vigil, making sure no one saw me. I quickly scoured the cab, looking to see if the driver was hunkered down there, asleep.

He wasn't.

He was probably still in the back.

I hoped he couldn't see me.

I pulled a clothes hanger out of the bag.

I had realized the other day that my basket handle was too small to fit over the large mirror on the driver's side. That was where I planned to leave the food, so he was sure to see it.

I had thought about tying it on with ribbon or string, but felt it would take too long. A hanger was perfect. I could slip the bag's handles over it, hang it off the metal part that attached the mirror to the truck, which would take seconds, then make a fast getaway.

Which was exactly what I did.

Done.

"All right," I whispered. "Let's go."

We took off fast, broke into a run, and headed to the path along the river all lit up with Christmas lights. My dog ran ahead to our favorite bench and after I brushed off the snow, I helped him up and we sat, snuggled together, once again staring up at the stars.

I sent out a silent prayer for the man in the truck, wishing my tiny act of love might spark hope in his heart, even for a moment.

Another shooting star exploded across the sky.

It was breathtaking and I was transported back to the night my mom and I had sat on this very bench together. It was during a meteor shower, and she had clapped with joy every time a streak of bright light illuminated the darkness. Every time I saw one, I thought of her. And luckily, I saw them often.

My heart burst with love.

"Thank you, Mom," I whispered. "For always being my inspiration."

Eventually, we made our way home.

Over the next couple of weeks, I felt driven to care for the camper driver and left him several items besides food, such as blankets, warm gloves, scarves, even money in case he needed a hotel room to shelter in, on exceptionally cold nights.

Then along came Christmas Day.

How awful to spend it all alone in a camper.

I'd gotten up early that morning and prepared two baskets. One I filled with Christmas food tucked inside a warming bag, slices of turkey, dressing, mashed potatoes. The other basket held wrapped gifts of socks, a book, and various items I thought he might need. I'd even created a multicolored beaded bracelet that spelled out 'you are loved' in gold. It matched my special rainbow Christmas card that read, "Never forget that you are loved."

"Merry Christmas," I whispered, after leaving the baskets, softly patting his truck.

I never saw the camper again.

One

Five years later

Jake Williams made it just in time.

For the past hour, snowflakes trickled down, but now pelted his truck in rapid succession, sticking to the windshield forming thick swirls of white crystals.

Clicking on his wipers revealed the town sign: Rainbow, Ontario. Population five hundred. It was different, newer than the one he remembered. The words and numbers were painted in florescent red under a stunning rainbow that conjured up magical thoughts of finding a pot of gold at the end of the multicolored arc.

He was finally there.

Sucking in his breath, he let it out slowly, unprepared for the wave of emotion sweeping through him. Wave? It was more like a tsunami. He'd expected to feel something, but not this. Sad, happy, fearful—he was experiencing them all, as if they'd united to effectively sucker punch him.

Sweat soaked his forehead as his breath quickened. His stomach rumbled. He felt ill. Shaky.

He had lived here twice before, both times briefly.

Once as a kid, another as an adult.

He'd always believed the town really was made of gold, for once upon a time he had felt loved there.

Eons ago.

Driving over the bridge leading to the center of town, Jake noted the large green wreaths adorned with shiny red and gold bulbs hanging from streetlights alongside the road. Wistfulness kicked in, especially since it was dark and they were all lit, twinkling, illuminating his path. Years ago, it had been a familiar sight and he remembered that folks here went all out to celebrate this festive season. He'd been so busy at work, he'd almost forgotten it was Christmas soon, but this town was certainly ready.

Slowing down, not wanting to miss the bed and breakfast sign, he peered through the falling snow. There it was—an arrow pointing to the Rainbow B&B. He braked, turned right, and pulled into the parking lot at the end of the cul-de-sac, slowing to a crawl before he stopped, making sure he didn't skid on the fresh snow. It was the only building on the small street and nostalgia hit again, as he remembered walking by this salmon-colored brick building as a child, wanting to climb up the stairs to the porch and plop down on their swing. It was bright red with big comfy blue cushions and had always looked inviting, but of course, it was nowhere to be seen in the middle of winter. Instead, a large six-seater red toboggan stood leaning against the wall, promising all sorts of winter fun.

Glancing at his watch, he wondered if seven a.m. was too early to sign in.

Only one way to find out.

Easing out of the truck, he stretched his arms and legs, stiff from the long drive. Reaching into the back seat, he picked up his backpack and headed up the stairs. Garlands of entwined greenery floated across the porch sporting red and gold bows. He remembered the town chose theme colors, and obviously, red and gold was it for this year. Green and silver had been on display his last Christmas there. The bed and breakfast festive presentation drew him in and, almost without knowing, a smile inched across his face as he pushed open the door.

The blond-haired woman behind the desk looked up from her computer and smiled. "Good morning. May I help you?"

"Hello there. Is it too early? Should I come back later?"

"Not at all. We welcome visitors at all hours of the day and night." She stood and reached out her hand. "I'm Holly Davis and I can help you get settled."

She had a Christmas name. How apt.

"Thank you, Holly." He shook her hand. "It's wonderful to see a smiling face. The name is Jake Williams and I booked a reservation for two weeks."

She glanced down as her hands flew over the computer keyboard.

"Certainly, Mr. Williams, I see it here. I've put you on the ground floor looking out at the river across the street." She picked up a key. "If you don't feel like joining in the Christmas festivities around here, you will at least be able to see all sorts of activities at the pavilion without even leaving your room. Come, follow me."

"Please, call me Jake," he said, as he hurried to keep up. She stopped beside a room labelled Candy Cane, opened the door, and handed over the key.

"Well, Jake, getting in the spirit, the rooms are all labeled with Yuletide titles. All you have to do is remember Candy Cane."

"What a great idea."

"Thanks. And please, let me know if you need anything."

"I will, thank you."

"By the way, there's a pamphlet on the night table with all the festive events going on." She grinned. "You mind find some of them interesting and catch a few."

"I'll be sure to take a look."

"Good." She started to walk away, then turned back. "You know, there was a Jake Williams who went to the elementary school here for a while. It wouldn't have been you, would it?"

"Yes, that was me. But I'm sorry, I don't remember a Holly Davis in my class."

"I was Holly Stuart back then, and I was a grade below you." She smiled. "Weren't you the one who took on the school bully who stole a knapsack? And you got it back?"

She remembered that?

"Stuart White. You saw me do that?"

"Yes, I was in the park with a whole bunch of my friends when you came running after him. You were our hero. Not only did you get the knapsack back, I heard you yell at him to stop bullying people or else you'd report him to the police. He was such a big guy, no one had ever stood up to him, and we saw how scared he looked." Her eyes took on a faraway look. "That kid was always stealing my lunch and my friend's food as well, so we started to do what you did and threaten to tell on him, and he stopped." She chuckled. "It turned out his dad was a cop and would have grounded him forever if he knew."

Jake smiled. "I'm glad to hear he stopped."

"It was all thanks to you. You were a legend to me and my friends."

A bell rang out.

"Oh, more customers. Gotta go, but we'll have to catch up later," she said, as she hurried to the front desk.

"I'd like that," he shouted as she ran down the hall. It was amazing to think he even knew the receptionist after all these years. Or she remembered him, was more the truth. A legend? Hardly. But he did remember Stuart White. He was glad to hear he had managed to straighten up.

He walked over to the window, happy he'd chosen a bed and breakfast rather than the hotel on the outskirts of town. It was warmer and homier and the path along the river was all lit with glowing stars, both real and artificial, and looked spectacular. He could even make out several people out for an early morning walk with their happy, prancing dogs.

Christmas really was here.

Jake and his brother Evan worked long hours with little time to celebrate important occasions. Or at least he did. His brother usually made it home to his family for supper, and always extended an invitation to Jake, who declined. He always spent Christmas Day at his desk with whatever takeout he could find, usually just a turkey sandwich, not in the mood to celebrate.

This was different.

He picked up the pamphlet listing all the local events, planning on attending every Christmas activity in town.

He was on a mission.

Anticipation rippled through him.

To find *her*.

His mystery woman.

Two

But first, breakfast.

Walking out the door, Jake waved at Holly who was busy talking on the phone, crossed the road and stood outside the restaurant door. It was still called the Sanctuary Breakfast Nook, nicknamed the Nook, and that was exactly what it had been for him back then, a refuge every morning during two weeks of unendurable pain. All created by himself.

Nerves rippled through him.

His breathing shot up.

Should he enter?

Would it be too painful dredging up the past?

But why come, then?

The whole point was that he was there to face his past. Then again, in thought form, it made sense, but being here made it real and not pleasant.

Oh, not that the restaurant wasn't pleasant; it just represented a time in his life of incredible unhappiness.

Just when he wanted to run away, two customers exited and

the smell of bacon wafting out set his stomach rumbling. He remembered the Nook served the best breakfasts ever.

He was going in.

Opening the door, he walked in to a colorful array of Santa Clauses on every available shelf, red cloths adorning each table, and tiny, twinkling, Christmas trees placed between the sugar bowls and salt and pepper shakers. Just how he remembered, for it was Christmas the last time he had been there, same as now. Nothing much had changed in five years, at least with the décor, which soothed his soul with its familiarity. He took a seat at a table by the window, his old seat, the one he used to use regularly.

“Coffee?” asked the waitress, appearing as if out of nowhere.

“Please.” Jake smiled as she righted the mug already on the table and poured from a silver carafe. “There’s nothing like the smell of coffee first thing in the morning. Thank you.”

“I agree, and you’re welcome. Would you like to look at a menu?” She held one out.

“No, thanks. Bacon and scrambled eggs will be fine.”

“Coming right up.”

Before the waitress turned away, he got a glimpse of her nametag. Kelly, it read. Just as he thought. She was the same one who had waited on him every day five years ago. Her hair was longer, slightly greyer, tied back and secured under a hairnet, but she had the same sweet smile and kind eyes. She didn’t recognize him, but he couldn’t expect her to. Back then, he’d had long shaggy hair, a scruffy beard, and rarely looked anyone in the eye. His appearance was vastly different now—short hair and clean shaven.

It was nice to see a familiar face.

As the room filled up, he slowly perused it, remembering they always had a crowd each morning. That hadn’t changed, either. The Santa decorations still amused him, for they were all different shapes and colors and many moved as they mechanically pushed gifts into bags, made a snowman, or traveled with reindeer. He checked to see if his favorite was there. Yes, it was. Santa kissing Mrs. Claus under the mistletoe. It always made him grin.

"Here's your order."

Head turned the other way; Jake hadn't seen her coming. He'd forgotten how fast their chef was and wondered if he was the same one.

"Thank you." Closing his eyes, he took a bite of the eggs. Awww...bliss. Still the best breakfast ever.

"Do I know you?"

He opened his eyes, unaware Kelly was still standing there, squinting at him.

He nodded. "Maybe. I used to come here years ago."

"I usually never forget a face, but you look different now." She leaned closer, then snapped her fingers. "Jake, right?"

"Yes." He was impressed.

"Your hair was longer and you had a beard."

"Great memory." He smiled as it hit him. Could *she* be the one he was looking for? Could it be that simple?

"Then you disappeared."

"Yes. I left for a new job." He shoveled down another mouthful of eggs. Just couldn't resist. He'd driven straight there, about a twenty-four-hour drive, and eaten little on the way. "Sorry for being rude. I'm just really hungry."

"Go ahead. I'm the one bothering you." She smiled, warm and friendly. Just as he remembered.

"You're not bothering me at all. It's nice to see a friendly face."

"Well, welcome back." She leaned down to top off his coffee. "Are you here to stay or just for a visit?"

"Just for a visit. I'll be around for a couple of weeks."

"You'll enjoy yourself. The whole town comes alive at Christmas."

"Yes, I remember." He bit into his toast. Homemade bread. He'd forgotten they baked it fresh every morning.

"Are you over at the Rainbow Bed and Breakfast?"

"I am."

"Great. Well, hope to see you again."

"Thank you and I'll be back." He laughed. "Probably every day."

"Good." She pointed to his plate. "Sorry. I'd better leave you to eat in peace."

"No problem. I'm enjoying reconnecting with you." Making conversation with locals was important to him. Especially if Kelly turned out to be who he was looking for. He watched her smile at everyone as she made her way to the kitchen. She certainly knew all the townsfolk. If it wasn't her, she may know who it was.

Jake dug into the rest of his food, savoring every bite, still convinced it was the best breakfast he'd ever had. Apparently, or what the table behind him was arguing about, it was to do with a special sauce they used in the eggs. They were probably right.

He thought about how far he'd come.

Definitely a long way.

The last time he'd been there, he was in rough shape. It had just been a place to park, drink, and wish his life away.

Don't dwell.

He needed to concentrate on his search, the reason for being there.

His brother Evan's face floated before him.

Jake was forever grateful his brother had welcomed and taken him in at his lowest point, even offering him a reporter job at the *Manitoba Times* which he owned and ran. Evan did everything he could to help him climb out of his depression. He was much better now, having seen a counselor on a regular basis, rented an apartment, and even though he was a lawyer, he had stayed a journalist, discovering he loved the hunt for a story.

Unfortunately, the paper wasn't doing well.

A rival had arrived in town and they were losing subscriptions by the dozens. The new paper relied on sensationalism and over-exaggeration, bordering on lies, to attract viewers. It was working.

Evan's work mission was devoted solely to reporting the news, not creating it, and was honest and truthful. No story appeared unless highly fact-checked, and the paper didn't have agendas targeting people. Or, destroying them with gossip. If they weren't sure, they didn't run it.

Sad that people often enjoyed the tabloid-style one.

Usually quick to grin, lately his brother's eyes were swamped with worry. He was facing having to lay off devoted employees and possibly shutting down completely.

Closing his eyes, Jake shook his head sadly, remembering their conversation a few days ago in the office.

"As you know, we've always been known for our post-Christmas edition," his brother had said. "It's by far the one we've sold the most copies over the years."

Evan was right.

The papers leading up to this special edition were filled with cookie recipes, baking and decorating the best Yule log and gingerbread house, the correct way to roast a tasty turkey, holiday-themed crosswords, and city events. Then came the post-Christmas Day edition, midway between Christmas and New Year, a collector's item, filled with many recent real-life Christmas miracles that touched the hearts of the townsfolk. But the showstopper, so to speak, was one main story that graced the front page, the one that had people talking for months. It was always extra-touching, boosting sales, making it the favorite paper of the year. Businesses ran extra advertisements and the end result was a thick, packed newspaper that people often kept as a memory over the years. Unfortunately, this year the reporter who hunted down the main story had retired unexpectedly and moved down south. Evan wasn't sure why, but wondered if job insecurity led to his leaving the paper in a hurry.

As of now, they had nothing.

They were stuck.

"I hate competing, but with the other paper growing in subscribers, we need a good one," Evan had continued. "Something that will remind people of who we are and make them believe in us again." He had then jumped up, snapped his fingers and said, "I know. You need to tell your story."

"My story?" At first, Jake didn't know what he was talking about.

"Yes. You told me a lot about that mysterious woman in Rainbow and how you always wanted to go back and find her." He paced back and forth, stopped, and stared at him. "Go look for her. Now. That would make a great story."

"Well, I would like to find her and have often thought of returning to track her down," he had said. "But to write an article in the paper about it? Bare my soul? No way." He had shaken his head emphatically to underscore his reluctance.

"Oh, go on, do it. You're good at searching out people. It'll probably just take a few days and you can stay longer and visit if you want. You haven't had a holiday in years.

His eyes popped open.

His brother had won.

Here he was in Rainbow, a town he hadn't visited for five years, on a search. Evan was convinced this story could save the paper, and Jake couldn't hurt or disappoint him, especially since he had helped him a lot. He had to at least try. It was out of his comfort zone to promise an article featuring himself, but he felt he had to do it.

It was a twofold mission.

First, it was obviously to help his brother. But it was also a personal quest to hunt down his mystery woman, someone he had never seen, at least clearly. He'd had only a fleeting glimpse of a slight figure in a black parka, hood up, walking a small black dog. He had heard the person call the dog, so he knew it was a woman, but didn't hear what name she had shouted out.

He had little to go on.

He didn't even know the color of her hair.

But he was determined.

Beginning now.

He glanced around the room again, looking to see if any of the women stood out to him.

Maybe she was right here? Eating breakfast as well.

Or maybe it really was Kelly.

The more he thought about it, the more he realized how much he wanted to find her.

No, he *needed* to find her.

After all, once upon a time, she had saved his life.

Three

After breakfast, Jake walked back to the Rainbow. Stomping the snow off his boots, he went in.

"Hi, again," Holly greeted him, pointing to the platter on the desk. "Would you like a cookie? They're fresh out of the oven."

He took a look. Gingerbread reindeer. It'd been a long time since he'd had one of those, or any Christmas cookie at all.

"Thank you." He picked one up and bit into it. "Excellent. Are you the baker?"

"Not on your life." She laughed. "My mother is the pro."

"Go ahead, take two." He turned to find a woman behind him. Tall, slim, blonde, with a smile that equaled her daughter's. Or he was pretty sure it was Holly's mother, since the resemblance was uncanny.

"You must be the baker." He reached out his hand for a shake.

"And you must be our new visitor. My daughter said you lived here a while back." She took his hand. "I'm Anna, Holly's mom, and go ahead." She pointed to the cookies. "Take several. I baked plenty."

"I think I will. One for later." He picked up another. "Thanks. And yes, I did live here for a year when I was ten."

"Well, welcome back. I believe once you've lived in Rainbow, you never forget it." Anna smiled. "I went to camp nearby as a child, and we used to hang around town a lot. I loved it here and vowed to come back one day, and here I am. A permanent resident."

"It certainly is a friendly town."

"That it is. By the way, do you have everything you need?" Anna asked. "Do you want more towels, for instance?"

"I'm good for now. Holly has been a huge help."

"Great." Anna beamed at her daughter. "Well, let us know if you need anything."

"I will, thank you."

Watching them both smile and seeing how kind they were, he wondered if maybe it was Holly he was looking for? Or, possibly her mother? Anna?

They both seemed to be the type of person to help others and they were within walking distance of where he'd once been. No dog, though, or at least one that he could see.

"You don't have a pet by any chance, do you?" He just had to know. It might narrow down his suspects. "Like a dog, for instance?"

"No," Holly answered. "Why? Did you hear barking last night? If so, it's probably coming from the path by the river. It's a popular place to walk a dog."

"I did hear barking." He didn't really lie. He had heard dogs playing over by the river. "It didn't bother me, though. I was just wondering if it came from here."

"It didn't, but one day I hope to have one."

"I doubt we'll get one, though," Anna added. "It's hard to have one around when you never know if your guests are allergic or just plain afraid of animals."

That was a good point.

Since part of his criteria was a dog, he could rule them out, but maybe not. Who knows, they could have been walking a friend's pup years ago. Or helping out a guest. Besides, they did seem to fit the characteristics he was looking for. He'd have to keep a close eye on them. He might have found his answer right where he was staying, instead of at the restaurant.

That'd be great.

Although Kelly was a good suspect, too. He wondered if she had a dog.

He walked down to his room, eyed the bed, and immediately yawned. Having a hard time keeping his eyes open, he napped. After all, he'd been up all-night driving. Besides, the snow hindered him from getting around easily and it'd be better when the town was plowed out.

Awakening a few hours later, he glanced out the window and saw only a few snowflakes drifting down, indicating the major storm was probably over. His next venture was to walk along the river, checking out the area, still figuring out a strategy for how to search out his mystery woman.

To be honest, he should have sorted that out before his arrival, but was caught up in trying to calm his brother instead. And during the long drive, his sole concern was navigating snow storms. Now here he was, finally in Rainbow. What did he expect? She'd just jump out in front of him?

Maybe.

Maybe she knew what he looked like.

Could be she might recognize him and give herself away. She'd obviously been worried about him, so she might be happy to see him looking better.

Then again, she might not have seen him at all. In fact, he doubted she had, since she moved in the dark when he was probably passed out. This was definitely going to be harder than he thought. Evan's sad eyes floated in front of him. But if it would save his brother's paper, he'd do anything. He was determined.

Bundling up, he stepped outside, sucking in the cold air and headed to the path, impressed it had already been shoveled. Relaxing, mentally enjoying the slower pace, he eyed the sparkly winter wonderland that surrounded him. Signature pops of gold and red were displayed on the gazebo decorated with green boughs and ribbons, and also seen on various trees, snowmen, and plastic reindeer. It was refreshing and soul-cleansing compared to the merry chase of stories he'd been working on the past month. He enjoyed writing, but at times the work weighed heavily on his mind and heart. Now was the time for a brief respite, for he was only going after one story, in one small town, albeit an important one, but it made a difference to how relaxed he felt.

Noticing a flickering delightful array of red, green, and silver colors, he realized a group of female power walkers was coming towards him, dressed for the festive season.

"Hello," he said, as they drew nearer. They all nodded and shouted out Merry Christmas, while he glanced at their smiling faces.

Was she one of them?

Was any of them the one?

Did someone recognize him?

Wait. What was this?

He looked down to see a little brown dog tugging at his pant leg, leash intact.

"Hi, there." He reached down to pick up the leash and patted the head of what looked like a young pup. The little guy wagged his tail, jumping up on him. "Where did you come from?" he asked. "Are you an escapee?"

"Charlie. Here." Then a more frantic, "Charlie, come back here."

Jake looked over to see a woman racing up the hill, her head twisting back and forth as she called again, "Charlie, where are you. Come here right now."

The little dog turned towards her and Jake said, "Are you Charlie?"

The pup wagged his tail even harder.

"Is this your dog?" Jake asked, walking towards her, the pup hurrying to greet her.

"Oh, yes," she gushed, rushing over and taking hold of the leash. "He's still young, not even four months old, but fast as lightning. He yanked his lead right out of my hand. Thanks for keeping him safe."

"No problem. He's a cute pup."

"He sure is." She picked him up and held him tightly.

Curious, he stared at the elfin face peeking out of her big, woolly white hat. Tears rolled down her cheeks. Obviously, the result of the fear of losing her dog.

What?

He took a step back.

In shock.

He knew her.

As a matter of fact, on his drive to Rainbow, he had wondered if he would run into her, although he wasn't sure if she still lived there. He'd thought about checking out phone records and addresses or asking Kelly or Holly, but in the end decided against it. After all, they hadn't left on good terms.

And there she was, right in front of him.

Unbelievable.

"Cassie Blackburn," he finally said. "It's really you."

He would never forget those bright blue eyes, sad now, and the blond curls that were flying around her face, courtesy of the wind. Way back when he knew her, her hair had been longer, a tangle of golden ringlets that flowed to her waist, and yes, he once had a huge crush on her. As much of a crush as a ten-year-old could have.

Memories surfaced.

He remembered his family moving to the house next door

and meeting her for the first time, where he was instantly mesmerized by her big, friendly smile and the fact she always looked at you as if you were the only one that mattered. She was kind and sweet and had walked with him on his first day of school and took the time to show him around. She had also made room for him at the lunch table and introduced him to all her friends. They were inseparable after that. Hanging together every moment they could.

Until he had left.

"Excuse me?" she asked, staring at him. "Do you know me?"

Her words pulled him out of his thoughts, and he opened his mouth to say his name when she said quickly, "Wait, I do know you. You're Jake Williams, who was my once-upon-a-time next-door neighbor."

"Yes, for a year, and we were in the same fifth grade together."

"And then you moved."

He was surprised to hear her words sounding harsh, as if angry. Was she? Nah. Couldn't be. After all, she was the one who had created the problem, not him.

"My dad got a new job, and off we went to Ottawa," he said.

"Have you moved back?"

Again, harsh.

"No, just here on vacation."

"Well, it is certainly the best time of the year to come. There's a lot going on."

She turned her head, as if about to leave. He was hoping she'd stay. "I wasn't sure if you still lived here," he said, trying to keep her there, wanting more time.

"I do. I never left." She shrugged. "I commuted to Marner University where I got my teacher's credentials, and now I teach grade eight at our old school, Rainbow Elementary."

"Really? They are lucky to have you."

"Well, I'm lucky to be there."

Her dog let out a little woof and started pulling. Cassie shook her head. "I really must work on leash respect from my pup, but I'd better go. I have a lot of errands to run. Besides, I think he's hungry. See you, and thanks again."

Shockingly, considering she'd been rather aloof, she reached her hand out for a shake.

"Good to see you again," he said, shaking her hand, which she pulled away fast, waving as she walked away.

Cassie Blackburn.

Why she was cool towards him was a mystery. After all, she was the one who had stopped all contact with him, which had broken his ten-year-old heart. He'd figured she'd just moved on, so he did the same, trying not to think of her. If anyone should be upset, it should be him. But of course, that was a long time ago. A lot had happened since then and it was ridiculous to hold a grudge.

Maybe it was a stroke of luck that he'd run into her.

He didn't plan on being friends again—after all; they lived quite a distance from each other, but if she had lived here her whole life, she probably knew everyone.

Maybe she could help him find who he was looking for. Or at least point him in the right direction of someone who might know.

He might have found the key to pinning down the person he searched for.

He hoped.

But he doubted it.

Judging by how she acted today, he was not in her good books, and she wouldn't go out of her way to help him.

Maybe she had just changed in general.

Could be she wasn't the nice person he remembered.

Or, maybe she was the one.

Aha! Another suspect.

Unlikely, though.

Four

"Hey, Charlie, no more running away from me."

Reliving the terror she'd felt when he had jerked the leash out of her hand, Cassie stopped for a moment, scooped him up again, and hugged him tightly.

"Don't do that anymore," she whispered. "I thought I'd lost you for good." Staring at his little face with his sparkling big eyes, she burst into laughter when he enthusiastically licked her, then squirmed to be put down. Placing him on the snow, he immediately rolled in it, ate a chunk of ice, twirled, then stopped to chase his tail round and round. He was such a happy puppy, she thought, and she was enjoying every minute as the two of them continued their trek home. This time she managed to keep his leash in her hand and, for part of the way, he trotted right beside her.

"Well done, sweetie. We'll figure this all out." She unhooked him in one of the fenced areas of her apartment building, pulled a ball out of her pocket, and let him romp freely chasing it. "There's a time to walk with me on a leash and a time to run like anything when safe."

Speaking of being safe, she was glad Charlie had escaped to someone who took care of him. But of all people, Jake Williams.

Jake.

Wow.

It had been years since she had last seen him.

Conjuring him up as a child, she recalled his mop of bright red hair that held daily duels with a comb. His hair usually won. He was always flicking it off his face and one day he showed up on her front porch with extra short bangs and a big smile. "I cut it off myself," he had said proudly, not caring that he looked comical with long hair and a teeny tiny fringe across his forehead. Stifling a giggle, she had assured him he looked good because that was what she liked best about him. He did what he had to do, regardless of what others thought.

Jake was a real individual.

And for sure, Cassie'd had a huge crush on him from the first moment she'd caught sight of him when they'd moved in. It was summer, and she had been sitting on her porch reading when she saw his mom struggle with a suitcase, trying to pull it out of the trunk of her car. Spotting her, Jake ran over and said, "I'll get it, Mom." Immediately, she figured he was a nice boy. A kind one. A 'good spirited' kid, as her own mother would say. Then one day he saw her playing hopscotch in front of her house, walked over, gave her a piece of his chocolate bar, and their friendship was sealed. They became best buddies and had even scratched Jake and Cassie – besties forever – on a bench in the school playground.

Charlie dropped the ball at her feet, and she picked it up and threw it again, watching him charge it, then toss it around with his paws.

But as well as remembering the fun times, she also remembered some sadder ones. She recalled as if it were yesterday, the moment she'd arrived home and while walking down the hallway to the kitchen, she'd overheard her mother tell her dad her new neighbors were struggling. Apparently, while hanging up the laundry in the back yard, she had seen Jake's mom sitting on a chair crying. Mom had gone over to see if she could help and found out Jake's dad had been laid off and they had moved here looking for work, thinking they had more opportunities in Rainbow than their last town. Times were tough for them, and money was scarce.

That was why Jake brought very little at lunch and sometimes didn't even have one, Cassie had figured. She used to give him her treat every day, telling him she just didn't want it. Sometimes she even offered her sandwich if she saw him with nothing, and when she mentioned this to her mom, she'd found extra sandwiches and goodies in her bag. She always pretended to Jake that she'd eaten a huge breakfast and wasn't hungry. It used to make her sad to see him wolf down the food as if he hadn't eaten in a while. It was probably true. He hadn't.

She also remembered the moment he broke her heart.

The two of them had hung together that whole day. They'd been at the park where they'd played on the slide and the teeter-totter and had races over who could swing the highest. On the way home, they'd stopped for ice cream, and then Jake had helped her rake the leaves in the back yard. The fact they'd jumped in them and had to rake them over again was a whole other story. They'd even pinky-sworn that they would stay best friends forever, no matter what.

Bam.

He was gone.

Two days later he had disappeared overnight with his family.

What was worse, he had never said goodbye or told her he was leaving or where he was going.

Cassie had been upset, and she'd moped around for weeks. Losing her best friend hurt badly but she also felt betrayed. After all, they had pinky-sworn, made a promise, and he'd broken it so fast her head spun. She'd thought of him often over the years, came close to looking him up on social media or trying to find him through internet searches, but instead gave up. What difference would it have made? It was clear he wanted nothing to do with her.

And here he was.

Back in town.

Charlie nudged her leg, yanking her out of her memories.

"Had enough, sweetie?" Even pups eventually tire. "C'mon, Charlie, let's go get you some breakfast. Panda will be wanting her food too."

At the mention of Panda, his tail wagged enthusiastically. He was madly in love with her fourteen-year-old cat, who she had taken in when her owner passed away. Panda loved exerting her seniority and enjoyed bossing the pup around, making sure Charlie knew who was in charge. Although the two were best buddies, Charlie's love for her was definitely the greater one. He wanted to be with her every moment, whereas Panda declared 'enough' and retreated to her many cat caves. Without a doubt, they were fun to watch with their individual personalities on display.

Cassie opened the door, and they walked up the steps to her apartment on the second floor. However, she still couldn't get Jake off her mind as his face floated before her again.

This time, as an adult.

He looked the same, except his hair was shorter and more of a deeper auburn color. It was not as tousled and had obviously developed a better relationship with a comb, but stuck up here and there, still asserting its independence. And she liked the fact his big, toothy grin hadn't changed. A part of her wanted to fall right back into the close friendship they once had, but nope, not this time. Cassie was keeping her distance. She didn't suggest they get together, and planned to avoid/ignore him if she ran into him over the next week. She wasn't going to set herself up for hurt again.

No way.

Walking into their apartment, they were greeted by Panda meowing loudly, just in case she'd forgotten she hadn't had breakfast yet. "Don't worry. I'll have it ready in a moment." She turned on her coffee machine, all prepared before she left, as she got her fur kids their food.

"There you go." She put the two bowls down beside the water dish.

Watching them devour it with gusto, she once again gave thanks that Charlie was safe.

She'd have to make sure he didn't slip away again. Unfortunately, she had gotten distracted thinking of the fundraiser she was in charge of and had been working out the details in her mind when he had tugged hard and escaped.

The fundraiser.

She poured herself a cup of coffee and sat at the kitchen table.

This event was coming soon, and she hoped everything was ready.

Shoving Jake out of her mind, Cassie thought about the conversation she'd had with her friend and fellow teacher, Jill Haley. Along with her husband, they ran the horse rescue farm outside of town called Joyful Second Chances. The work they did was spectacular and awe-inspiring, saving abandoned horses, nurturing and rehabilitating them. Since Jill was an accomplished equestrian, they also offered riding lessons, free for those who couldn't afford to take them. Cassie admired Jill immensely, but noticed her friend seemed sad lately and finally got it out of her that the cost of medical bills and food was astronomical and, unfortunately, way beyond their budget. They needed money, stat, to care for the horses they had, and especially to take in more rescues, for there always seemed to be plenty of them. They were even facing bankruptcy if things didn't improve.

Cassie wanted to help. She'd been mulling over what she could do when one of her grade eight students, Riley Asher, came up with the idea of the fundraiser.

Good for Riley.

Turned out she helped out at the farm, was an avid horse rider, and one morning had burst into the classroom, sat quickly, and frantically waved her arm.

"Yes?" Cassie had asked.

"My mom told me Second Chances needs help. Please, please, can we organize a fundraiser?"

Riley's mom was a friend of Jill's as well, and obviously Riley knew the truth. She spoke with such passion that the whole class had erupted in screams of yeses and loud claps of excitement. After all, she had taken them there several times for riding lessons.

Cassie had been thinking along similar lines, but when an idea came from the students, it would be a guaranteed success. No doubt about it. She'd discovered over the years that when young people decided to do something themselves, their energy held no limits.

It had just taken fifteen minutes to pick a date—Christmas Eve day—the only time the school gymnasium was available. They had also chosen a name—Joyfest, in honor of the farm's name, but also in remembrance of the first horse Jill had taken in, who, of course, was named Joy. As Riley summed up, "And joy is what we are trying to bring to these horses." She was right.

Smiling, she watched Charlie curl up on his dog bed, eyes finally closed. Panda headed off to her favorite resting spot, Cassie's bed. Charlie knew enough not to follow her there or he'd be swatted off. That was Panda's cherished special place, and she wasn't sharing. At least yet.

Time to get some work done.

Pulling out her notebook, she checked off everything they'd accomplished so far. Rushing to get the fundraiser organized, her whole class had already gathered numerous sponsors, donations, and found plenty of vendors who were willing to give their profits to the farm.

Cassie couldn't wait.

Her heart went out to all the horses in need who deserved a second chance. They should experience joy, everyone should, and she was going to do all she could to help them.

Forget about Jake. He wasn't worth a second thought.

Five

Time to do some serious sleuthing.

Days were flying by, and Jake had nothing. He had a lot of suspects, but not even a hint of who it could be.

First, back to where it all began.

Who knew? Maybe the woman still walked her dog there.

The next day at five in the morning, Jake bundled up and poured himself a cup of coffee from the coffeepot always brewing in the foyer of the bed and breakfast. Grateful lids were provided to keep it from spilling, he then drove to the plaza where the restaurant was. Five years ago, he'd camped all over town, but this had been his main resting place. Fortunately, the exact spot where he used to park his camper stood empty. Not really unusual, since it was early and the whole parking lot was pretty bare. He pulled in, turned off the engine, and sat sipping coffee.

Imagine, five years ago, in this very spot, he was a mess.

A drunken, spaced-out mess.

Pain swallowed him.

The kind that tore at your heart and destroyed your mind.

He'd been avoiding it since he'd arrived.

This time, he allowed it.

Closing his eyes, he summoned up the long hours he'd spent there, mostly drunk. He hadn't wanted to face the fact he was jobless, moneyless, and homeless. All of his own making. The only reason he had lots of booze on hand was he once had a fully stocked wine cellar, which then lived in his camper.

The last time he'd been there, it was December also, and sometimes so cold he had piled on sweaters under his coat and had to start the truck several times to keep warm. But only for a short time, for he was always low on gas.

Mostly, he didn't want to acknowledge that someone had lost their life.

All because of him.

Oh, people tried to tell him it wasn't his fault, but he knew the truth—it was.

It had taken a long time and many counseling sessions before he realized it really wasn't.

But he was a wreck back then. Hiding from the world. Every single second an ordeal. He avoided everyone and hid in his truck. Booze was his only friend.

Jake took a deep breath and let it out slowly, trying to calm his racing heart. Opening his eyes, he gulped down the rest of the coffee and put the cup in the holder. He felt like he was there again, reliving how horrid it was, feeling shaky, knowing one thing for sure: he never wanted to live like that again.

But he couldn't stop thinking of the day the mystery woman appeared.

He had awakened, hung over, and found sandwiches and cookies in a pink basket swinging off his driver side mirror on a hanger. At first he was terrified, afraid someone knew he was camping out there, would tell the plaza owner, and he'd be kicked out. However, a note tucked in amongst the food read, 'You are loved.' That didn't sound like the kind of person who was out to get him and he really enjoyed the sandwiches and treats.

That night, he'd hung the empty basket out on the hanger, so if his mystery helper walked by, they could take it. The basket was quite spectacular and looked like it might cost a lot and he felt he should return it. But instead, they filled it again with more sandwiches. Next, he kept the basket, hoping they wouldn't feel obligated to leave anything, but another one, a green one, appeared with treats, a warm blanket, along with a gift card to the restaurant.

Tears trickled down, then and now.

He had heard when you hit rock bottom, genuine compassion could rock your world and save you, and now he had experienced it firsthand. He would never ever forget such kindness.

But it was Christmas that year that changed him forever, for on that day, he had experienced what he termed three miracles.

Jake could still summon up how he had been dreading that day.

He had hated being all alone.

He could have gone to his brother's, but he was a mess and didn't want Evan to see him like that.

So he'd drunk even more, hoping he'd sleep the night and day away.

He didn't.

A noise startled him awake and he looked out to see a woman running away, dog in tow.

Checking his mirror, he saw two baskets hanging there. Two hangers banged together in the wind, creating the noise he had heard.

Aha! That had been his mystery person. A few minutes earlier, and he might have seen her face.

The first amazing miracle was that his mysterious benefactor had left a full Christmas dinner in one basket, plus a series of small gifts in another. One gift was a homemade bracelet with the words 'you are loved' interwoven in gold among the multi-colored beads.

Pulling up his sleeve, he opened his eyes and touched the bracelet wrapped around his wrist. He had worn the bracelet every single day since, reminding him of the moment that had changed his life.

Back then, he had scarfed down the food, grateful for each bite. Then he had just sat, staring at the bracelet like he was doing right now, and at the words 'you are loved.' Much to his surprise, slowly, softly, gently, streaming out of a messed-up heart and a clouded, hung-over brain, a glimmer of hope had surfaced. Suddenly it had become clear to him that if a complete stranger could care for him, why couldn't he?

Maybe he really was worth saving.

There had to be another way for him besides alcohol.

At that moment, he vowed to himself that instead of spending the day drinking, he was going to get help, to stop killing himself with booze, and to join the land of the living once again— get well, get a job, and get stable.

He would view it as a new beginning. After all, wasn't Christmas all about rebirth? How apt that he would begin today.

Step by step, he'd get it together.

Or at least that was what he had promised himself.

But as the day rolled on, haunting memories surfaced, and he weakened.

He craved whiskey.

The second miracle was, fearing he'd give in and start drinking, he had swallowed his pride and called Evan, with the excuse of wishing him a Merry Christmas. What he really wanted was to just hear his voice. To his surprise, his brother cried when he realized who it was. He begged him to come visit, offered him a job and a place to stay. He said he missed him and so did his wife and their children.

Evan's children.

His two nephews.

Brad and Bailey. Five-year-old twins.

Apparently, they missed their Uncle Jake and kept asking for him.

He missed them, too.

Jake remembered the last time he'd seen them, probably a year ago, when they had visited. He had tucked them in bed, was conned into reading them five stories, and when they had fallen asleep, he had kissed each one on their forehead. He loved them with all his heart and had also felt loved by them and that day, Christmas Day, moved by the genuine caring in Evan's voice, he promised to drive to Manitoba and take him up on his offer.

He had hurt people he loved and it had to stop.

Now.

Calling Evan had been a good thing and after he hung up, he had gathered up the remaining bottles of alcohol, put them in a box, carried them over to the restaurant's back door, knocked loudly and run. Hiding behind a tree, he saw a worker open the door and carry it in.

Good, it was gone. All he felt was relief.

Sitting back in his truck that day, he was soon to experience his third miracle.

But first, another major problem.

How in the world could he get enough money for the gas needed to get to his brother?

Looking at his gas gauge, he realized he had only half a tank.

That was it.

His brother had offered to send money, but he couldn't bring himself to accept it. He knew they lived paycheck to paycheck and would have spent any extra on the boys for Christmas gifts.

Maybe the restaurant would let him wash dishes for a few days. However, he looked a mess, hadn't shaved in weeks, and his clothes smelled. He didn't even have the money to clean up.

Speaking of cleaning up, he decided he should tidy up his truck. It looked like a cyclone had hit, and besides, it would keep him busy and not thinking of drinking again. As he emptied the baskets, a card fell out.

What was this? He hadn't noticed it before.

When he opened it, two one-hundred-dollar bills slid out.

In case you need some spare cash, the note said.

Unbelievable. It was enough to get him to Manitoba, or at least close enough.

All he could think about was, *three miracles in a day*. It must be fate.

Filling his tank immediately, he had set out that very day.

And the rest was in his past.

But he thought of that mystery woman every single day.

He wanted to thank her for giving him his life back. In truth, he doubted he would have come to Rainbow again if it weren't for Evan. Being here really was bittersweet. It reminded him of happy times, but it was also where he had collapsed and fallen apart, not a great memory to hang onto. But now was his chance to find that lady and tell her what she had done for him. She deserved the best and all sorts of thanks and recognition for her good-heartedness.

His brother did, as well.

And that was the real reason he was there. To give back to Evan, who had given him everything.

Opening his eyes, he eagerly searched his surroundings.

Could it be possible he would find her right here? With a dog?

Did she have a routine?

Maybe. Maybe not.

Could be she just noticed the camper and came early to avoid interaction. He never really knew when she made an appearance, since he was always passed out in the back. And he had only caught a brief glimpse of her once.

Wait.

Was that Cassie?

Six

Jake leaned forward just as the woman dropped a handful of papers, and he caught a glimpse of her face. Yes, it was Cassie. Unhooking his seatbelt, he jumped out and ran over to help. As he reached down, she did as well. They bumped arms.

"Oh, no!" she cried, as the coffee in her other hand flew all over his jacket.

Grabbing the papers faster so they wouldn't get wet, he said, "Sorry about that. I was just trying to help."

"Oh, I'm the one who needs to be sorry." She straightened up. "I just ruined your jacket. Oh, it's you, Jake."

"Don't worry. It's nothing that soap and water can't handle. And yes, it's me." He rose as well and glanced at the papers he had gathered up that somehow managed to remain dry. "Come to Joyfest," he read out loud. "A chance to save Joyful Second Chances' Horse Farm." Eyebrows raised, he looked at Cassie. "I remember this place. Our class went riding there. It needs to be saved? Why? Is it in danger of closing?"

"Yes. If they don't bring in more money, they will have no choice. They'll be able to just about take care of the horses they already have but won't be able to help others. And there are many to save. My class is holding a fundraiser for them."

"Really?" Memories of the farm were vivid. He had spent some wonderful times there and he was shocked it might be shutting down to other rescues. They were doing good work with the horses. "Is there anything I can do?"

She squinted with an expression that could only be termed leery. Had he overstepped? After all, he hadn't seen her in years, and she wasn't overly warm when they had met the other day. Was he butting in where he didn't belong?

"Oh, please forget I said anything. See you." He turned to head back to his truck.

"Um, you'd want to do that?" she called out.

He looked back, surprised at her question, or even the fact she responded. "Yes, of course. I'm a big fan of the farm. I'm only here a short while, but if there is anything I can do, I'd like to get involved."

"Well," she shrugged. "I got permission from the stores earlier and could use your help to put these posters up. I have a ton of them and a lot of space to cover."

"Of course. I'd be happy to do that."

"Well. Come on, then." She handed him a roll of tape.

Together they scoured the mall, placing posters on every store window, tree, and post. And there were a lot of them. Surprising, especially since Cassie didn't seem too thrilled to renew her acquaintance with him, they worked well as a team, quietly focused, and were finished fast. He kept his mouth mostly shut, which seemed to help the situation.

"Since I ruined your coffee, can I buy you another?" he asked. He couldn't resist suggesting this, since he was enjoying being around her again.

She hesitated, and he expected her to say no. "All right. Actually, I'm starving." She glanced at her watch. "And my pup was fast asleep when I left, which means he's good for another hour. I have time."

Jake was surprised she accepted. "Is the Nook okay with you?"

"Sure. It's my favorite breakfast spot."

They walked over to the restaurant. Again, Jake stayed quiet, afraid he'd offend her somehow and send her running. Entering, they picked a booth near the window. Kelly came right over. "Coffee?" she asked.

"Yes, please." Jake nodded.

She filled his mug and looked at Cassie. "And a vanilla latte for you?"

"I'd love one." Cassie smiled. "You know me well."

Jake couldn't stop staring. He used to live for those smiles.

"I should. You've been getting one every morning for years." Kelly laughed. "Now, I know Jake here wants bacon and eggs. How about you, Cassie?"

"I'll have the same, thanks."

"Coming right up."

After she left, Cassie continued smiling. "I'm hooked on lattes."

"Good. If you enjoy them, why not?"

"Well, my father laughs at me. He thinks people mess around too much with their coffees. It should always be taken black, is his theory."

"My brother would agree. Not me, though. I enjoy experimenting. How is Adrian doing?" He remembered Cassie's dad as a hardworking man who always had time for his family. He used to watch them play ball in the back yard and he envied their closeness. His dad was rarely home and when he was, he seemed to want nothing to do with his kids.

"Dad's doing just great. He sold the hardware store and they're off traveling down east. Right now, they're on Prince Edward Island."

"Good for them. But I heard they got a lot of snow lately."

"Well, they're avid cross-country skiers. Snow is heaven to them."

"Will they make it home for Christmas?"

"They sure will. It wouldn't be the same without them."

"Here's your latte," Kelly said, placing the frothy mug in front of Cassie. "And your breakfasts." She had managed to carry both plates on one hand and delivered them easily.

"Thanks," Jake and Cassie said together, then laughed.

"I have never developed the knack of carrying two plates at the same time. You amaze me," Cassie added.

"It's a skill," Kelly said, as she poured more coffee into Jake's mug. "Also, years of practice."

"Oh, I know for a fact it's not your only skill," Cassie said. "You're one of the kindest people I know."

She was? Jake thought. Interesting to know it was not just his own opinion.

"Right back at ya," Kelly said, then took off to serve a group of people who had just arrived.

"Do you remember Saint Patrick's Church?" Cassie asked.

"I do. It was not far from where we lived."

"Kelly takes extra food there from the restaurant every single day," Cassie said. "And Reverend Tom distributes it to those in need here and in neighboring towns."

"That is definitely kind of her. But I remember you being like that, too. And you were only ten."

He recalled she used to bake muffins and distribute them to neighbors up and down the street. He assisted her occasionally and many offered money, but she wouldn't take it. "I'm just trying to brighten up your day," she'd say.

"You remember the baked goods?" Her face turned red, a habit when embarrassed.

"Of course. And also, the happy faces of the neighbors who received them."

"Where do you live now?"

Jake grinned, knowing she was changing the topic, getting the focus off herself. She never liked to be the center of attention back then, and it looked like she still felt that way.

"In Manitoba. My brother owns the local paper, and I work for him as a reporter."

"Really." She paused, taking a sip. "Best latte ever."

"Best breakfast, too."

"I agree."

They ate in silence for a while.

"It must be exciting reporting the news," Cassie said, finishing her toast.

"It is. I enjoy writing and the hunt for the story."

"What brings you back here?"

Should he tell her?

Would she think he was insane coming all this way to root out a mystery giver from five years ago?

Then again, she might be able to help.

Even better, what if she was the one? She was certainly kind enough to do something like that, or at least that was how he remembered her. He doubted it at first when they had reconnected, based on how cool she'd been to him in the park, but seeing her trying to save the horse farm showed she was still probably one of the most generous people he'd ever known. And Kelly had confirmed that.

Deciding to take the chance, he told her about his mission, watching her eyes closely to see if she reacted in any way, indicating she might know something.

She didn't, but she did place her hand on top of his. He liked that. A lot.

"I'm sorry you went through this. And alone," she said.

He sensed she meant it, too.

"Well, I did have help from that anonymous person."

He rolled up his sleeve and showed her the multi-colored beaded bracelet left by his helper, with the words 'you are loved' on it.

"Do you recognize this, by any chance?"

He held his breath, hoping she'd say yes. Or at least give him a clue who could have made it or if it was purchased somewhere she knew.

She leaned closer and studied it, even ran her fingers over the words. "No, sorry. Can't help you."

"Oh, well. It was worth a try. If you think of anyone it could be, would you let me know?"

"Maybe." She frowned. "It's wonderful that she helped you, but what if the person doesn't want you to know?"

"Well, I think she'd be interested in finding out how she literally saved my life."

Cassie shook her head again, this time vehemently, her ponytail swinging wildly.

"Maybe. Maybe not. If she had wanted you to know who it was, why didn't she just knock on the truck's door and ask if you were okay?"

"Maybe she was afraid to."

"Wait a second." She leaned forward. "You're a reporter. You're not writing a story about this, are you?"

He nodded. "I'd like to. My brother thinks it'll make a great Christmas inspirational story."

"I don't. It's sad you were down, but if she wanted you to know her identity, as I mentioned before, she would have made herself known."

"Oh, well, you're probably right." He didn't want to dwell on this, especially seeing Cassie looking upset. He had been enjoying their truce, or at least the fact she was friendlier towards him. He quickly said, "I think I'll pop out to the horse rescue farm. I'd love to see it again after all these years."

"I'm visiting there tomorrow." She paused. "Would you like to come along for the ride?"

"I'd like that." He was surprised she'd invited him. This blowing hot and cold was confusing.

"Would you mind if I added my number to your phone?" she asked.

"Not at all." He handed it over.

"There you go," she said, sliding it across the table. "I have a few things to do, but I'll call you with a time."

"I look forward to that."

She insisted they each pay for their own breakfasts and when they walked out of the restaurant, she said goodbye fast and took off in the opposite direction he was going.

Watching her practically run away, he smiled. She was always in a hurry back when they hung around, except right now she was probably running from him. But it sure felt good to be with her again. It was like he'd never left.

Walking back to the bed and breakfast, he reflected on their chat. He was still surprised how strongly she had reacted to his wanting to thank the person who had helped him. Could she have been the one who'd given him the gifts? Nah. She hadn't displayed any emotion at all when he showed her his bracelet. Surely, she would have given away something if she were the one. Unless she knew all along it had been him in that truck. No. She would have tried to talk with him if that were the case.

He was still going to keep an eye on her, though.

Then again, it could be Kelly.

Or Holly. Or Anna.

Just about anyone, at this point.

He needed to narrow it down somehow.

Seven

Text messages flew back and forth until Jake and Cassie settled on a time to visit Joyful Second Chances Farm. They also agreed to go in Cassie's car since she knew the way. Jake hadn't been there in years and could barely remember where it was, besides out in the country somewhere.

He couldn't wait.

Walking over to the restaurant, he was eager to eat breakfast, then meet up with Cassie. Hanging at the farm was a happy memory he was looking forward to reliving.

He opened the door and Kelly approached him, always smiling.

"The usual?" she asked.

"Definitely, thank you." He settled down at his favorite table, where she filled his mug and took off fast. Once again, Jake was impressed that she greeted everyone by name and was definitely well-liked for he also noticed that customers spoke to her with real warmth. She always asked how their kids were, how their jobs were going, and seemed to know numerous details of their lives. She had probably grown up with a lot of them and seemed to genuinely care about each one of them.

Was it time to ask her about the mysterious stranger who had helped him?

If he were too open, he worried his search would spread around town and people might clam up. He already knew from living there that news traveled fast, but on the other hand if he didn't ask, he wouldn't find out anything. And he had little time to waste.

Would she know something?

She might, since she seemed to be aware of all the town's goings on.

And if she was the one who did it?

Would she admit it?

Would his search end here? Just like that?

"Here you go." Kelly placed his plate on the table and filled his mug for the second time. "The cook saw you come in, and had it ready fast."

"Thank you."

Say something.

Should he?

No.

Yes.

No.

She left to serve another table, but that was okay. He had chickened out anyway. Instead, he concentrated on eating, or practically inhaling his food. It was delicious.

"Sorry, I've been really busy this morning."

Startled, Jake looked up to see Kelly was back. He hadn't seen her approach; he'd been immersed in savoring every bit of his breakfast.

"Oh, don't worry," he said. "I can see all the tables are filled."

"How are you doing?" She leaned down to top up his coffee.

"Thank you. I'm doing great. It's good to be back."

"I can imagine. Rainbow gets in your blood."

She seemed to have a moment of respite, the perfect opportunity. “Kelly,” he burst out. “Would you mind if I ask you something? A serious question?”

“Of course not. Spill it.” She put the pot on the table, resting her hands on her hips. “Go ahead.”

“Well, when I was here the last time, five years ago, I’m sure you noticed I was in rough shape.”

She reached down and patted his hand. “I did. I just figured you were going through a hard time.”

“I was. And someone left baskets of goodies hanging on my truck.” He watched her closely, noting a smile forming, then quickly disappearing.

“That was nice. Did you see who it was?”

“No, not clearly. I saw a woman and a dog, but not her face.”

“Were you happy with the gifts?” Her eyes narrowed, and she tapped her fingers on the table as if impatient for his answer.

“Yes, of course. It was very kind.”

She smiled. “And were the baskets all different colors? And were there cards in them with a rainbow and the words ‘you are loved’ on it?”

That surprised him. How did she know such detail? Was she actually the one? Did she do this all those years ago?

“Yes. It was exactly as you said.”

“Well, you just got ‘rainbowed’.” She clapped her hands in excitement.

What?

“Rainbowed?” His eyebrows tightened together in confusion. “What does that even mean?”

“We have a mysterious helper in town, who every once in a while leaves baskets in rainbow colors with rainbow cards. Since Rainbow is the name of our town and conjures up joy and happiness and all good things, someone nicknamed what he or she did as getting ‘rainbowed.’ It stuck.”

It wasn’t just him? This woman helped many people? That

was amazing. It made him want to track her down even more. And it should be easier if she affected a lot of people. Hopefully.

He leaned closer. “Do you know who it is?”

He was positive he saw a flicker of recognition in her eyes before she looked down and picked up her coffee pot.

“No, sorry, I don’t.”

“Is it you?” He decided to just go for it.

This time, their eyes locked.

“No, of course not.”

But she sounded too emphatic, as if she were protesting too much.

“Do you have a dog?” He couldn’t resist asking.

She backed away. “Yes, but it’s not me, and I have no clue who it could be.”

“But surely someone must know.”

“Maybe.” She shrugged. “But I doubt it. I didn’t even know it was a woman until you mentioned it.”

Yeah, right.

“Really?”

“Yes, gotta go.” She turned and practically ran away. Then suddenly she appeared again. “Never forget that the legend is that it’s anonymous. Folks around here don’t go trying to figure it all out. I suggest you leave it alone.” She left again.

He had been ‘rainbowed.’

As if the giver were telling the person receiving the goodies that even amid hardships, they are the pot of gold. Which, in fact, was how he felt being the receiver of such kindness.

‘Rainbowed.’

And Kelly termed it a legend.

This was even bigger than he thought, and the more he focused on it, the more it aptly described what had happened to him. And it made for a better story, since it seemed to involve many people, not just him.

It had to be Kelly. She knew too many details and was also warning him off, inferring that people wouldn’t appreciate him snooping. She was now at the top of the list of suspects. He also realized he knew little about her. Did she live alone with her dog? Was she married? With children? Of course, that was really none of his business, but his curiosity had now really been piqued.

Glancing at his watch, he saw he had no more time to spend thinking about it. Cassie would be by soon. After paying the cheque and leaving a hefty tip, he walked back to the bed and breakfast to wait in his room.

Kelly.

It had to be.

Eight

Back in his room, Jake stood at the window watching for Cassie's car.

There it was.

Throwing on his coat, he rushed out to greet her.

"Wait a second," Holly said, coming out from behind her desk. She picked up a bag and a tray of drinks. "I've packed some goodies for you and Cassie."

Oh, right. He'd forgotten he'd told her where he was going and with whom.

"I also added a dog biscuit for Charlie. Homemade right here in Rainbow."

"Thank you." He peeked in the bag. "Cookies. My favorite. You're incredible, Holly."

"Well, Cassie is one of my most favorite people and you're my childhood hero. You deserve some special treats."

"That's very thoughtful. Thanks."

Holly grinned at him as he waved goodbye, picked up the drinks, and hurried out the door.

"Good morning, Cassie," he said, pulling open the passenger door. He heard a bark and laughed. "And good morning to you too, Charlie. I come bearing hot chocolate, gingerbread snowmen, and a dog biscuit for the pup." He glanced at Cassie. "Is it okay for him to have it? Holly, the receptionist, said they're homemade here in town and the package mentions the baker is a woman who specializes in healthy dog treats."

"That would be Margie Wilson. Sure, Charlie'd love one."

Jake sat, shut his door, quickly opened the dog cookie packaging, reached back, and handed Charlie the cookie.

Cassie laughed. "He'll be your best friend from now on."

"I'd love nothing more. Would you like one now as well? Gingerbread, I mean, not a dog cookie."

She laughed. "Thanks, but I'll wait." She sipped her hot chocolate as she pulled out to the road. "Holly and Anna always serve the best chocolate and make the best cookies."

"They sure do. Anna, the owner, and the baker, reassured me that at Christmas, cookies for breakfast are okay." He took a bite, savoring the taste. "It's my dessert after bacon and eggs."

Cassie laughed. "I agree with Anna. Tis the season for all the rules to just fly away."

"Holly was a grade behind us. I don't remember her."

"Yes, she was. She was really quiet back then and shy as anything."

"Really? Well, she's great with us customers at the bed and breakfast." He took another bite, figuring he could chomp on the cookies all day long.

"She's not shy anymore, loves running the bed and breakfast, and is involved in all sorts of volunteer work." Cassie glanced at him. "She's pretty incredible."

"I agree. She certainly takes good care of me and is very free with the cookies." He paused, then added, "Oh, by the way, have you ever heard of the saying 'you've been rainbowed?'" After talking to Kelly, he figured it was time he started asking around. Subtly. And maybe to just a few selected people. If he didn't, he'd be gone soon without discovering anything. Cassie would probably know, having lived there her whole life.

Silence.

Guess he had been rather abrupt. It was on purpose, though. Sometimes surprising someone made them inadvertently blurt out the truth, or at least not be as guarded.

"Did I say something wrong?" He hoped not. Then again, maybe she was the one who had 'rainbowed' him. Was that why she was quiet?

"Ahhh...no, not at all. You just startled me by changing the subject so fast." She took another sip of chocolate. "I have heard that saying, but I don't know anything about it. Hey, speaking of this great season and special yuletide cookies, do you mind if I put on some Christmas carols? I listen to them every chance I get, leading up to the big day."

Now, she changed the subject. Fast. Just like he had. She also spoke slowly, as if carefully measuring her words. She definitely knew more than she had let on, but he wasn't going to push. Could be she really was the one who helped him all those years ago? She looked over at him, eyebrows raised, and he realized he hadn't answered.

"Please, go ahead." She flipped on the radio and turned the dial until Christmas songs came on. He hadn't heard any carols in years and enjoyed hearing her sing along. Then Charlie joined in with an occasional howl and they both erupted in laughter.

"What can I say?" Cassie said. "He loves to sing. Or howl is more like it. C'mon, join us."

"Well, I don't have as good a voice as the two of you, but why not?" He jumped in, embarrassed he didn't know most of the lyrics to "Rudolph" but, at least, he tried hard. And he was grateful when Charlie drowned him out, so Cassie just might think he knew more than he did.

Singing loudly and unashamedly, they drove outside the town limits, then turned down a long laneway heralding a sign with a beautifully painted chestnut horse. Across the top read: Joyful Second Chances Horse Rescue. Further down, several red barns came into view.

"They've certainly expanded since I was a kid," he noted. "I remember just one barn back then."

"Yes, they have. There are a lot of horses to rescue, and they've also taken in several dogs and cats. Or in truth, people keep dropping animals off." She pulled to a stop outside the farthest barn. "The owners said for us to meet them here."

"This looks like the original building."

"You're right. It is. They've turned part of it into an office."

He looked around. "The trees, the bushes, the trails. It all brings back memories of our class trip all those years ago. Good memories, too."

"Really? Um, didn't you fall off your horse?" He noticed she was stifling a giggle.

"Oh, all right. Yes, I did." He smiled. "I should have guessed you'd remember that. But in my defense, they gave me one of the biggest horses ever. Clyde was his name."

"Oh, yeah, blame the horse." This time she laughed out loud – a huge infectious belly laugh – and he joined in, recalling landing in the mud. He wasn't hurt, just humiliated. Looking back, it was rather funny.

"It was the grin on your face that made it all so hilarious," she added. "There you were, covered in mud, with the biggest, toothiest smile I'd ever seen."

"Hey, it was my first time on a horse. I was having fun."

"You sure were. And I'm amazed you still remember the horse's name."

"Of course, I do. Clyde was my buddy, and if I recall correctly, you were the one who grabbed some paper towels and helped clean me up." He looked over. "And you even pulled a spare t-shirt out of your backpack and gave it to me to replace my muddy one."

"No way. I was never that kind to you. It must have been someone else," she joked.

"It was you. I'm sure of it."

She looked around. "You know, I still bring my classes here."

"Go ahead, change the subject. I'll go along with it." He looked around as well. "Your students must love it. Even though I was a muddy mess that first time, I had a good time and particularly enjoyed brushing the horses after."

"Me too. It's a nice bonding time, rubbing the horses down. My students love it as well." The office door opened. "Oh, there's Jill now."

A tall woman stepped out, probably in her fifties, sporting a brown cowboy hat, her long hair twisted back in a ponytail. A huge grin spread across her face as she walked towards them, waving.

"I recognize her," he said. "Wasn't she a teacher at the school, too?"

"Yes, and she still is. She has the class right across the hall from me."

They got out of the car, Cassie opening the back door for Charlie.

After introductions, they all walked into the office.

Fast as lightning, a tiny beagle who'd been snoozing in a dog bed off to the side barked and ran straight to Jake.

"Who's this?" he asked, hunkering down to pet the pup who was wagging his/her tail, seemingly very glad to see him as if they were old friends.

"That's Gladys," Jill said. "She was left at our gate with a letter giving us her name, that she's five months old, and the owner apologizing for not being able to keep her."

"She certainly loves you," Cassie said. Even Charlie looked spellbound at the pup's instant liking of Jake.

"The feeling's mutual," he said, scooping the tiny dog up in his arms.

"She's a cutie and has only been with us for a few days," Jill said. "You know, Cassie, I just got a call this morning about two more horses who need rescuing, so I really appreciate you doing this fundraiser. Sometimes the demand for horse rescues is overwhelming."

"No problem," Cassie said. "Anything to help. But don't forget, it was a student who came up with the idea. She deserves all the credit."

"Right, Lainey. But I know you're the one overseeing it."

"Actually, not really. My kids have been amazing."

Jake was used to this side of Cassie. She never took credit for what she did but passed it on to others. His heart jumped a beat as he found himself warming towards her. It was as if all those years had disappeared, and they were best buddies again. The thought made him feel good.

"But I wanted to touch base with you." Cassie continued. "Besides raising money, which we're trying to do, you once mentioned other ways people can help out here?"

"Yes. I've been thinking it over and was going to call you about this," Jill said. "I'm glad you dropped by. Obviously, general donations are important, but sometimes people might be more interested in sponsoring a horse for a year or longer. We would send them monthly newsletters about their horse, including photos, and they can visit whenever they want. Or they can buy a bale of hay or several of them, medicine, or even volunteer. All of that helps."

"Great," Cassie said. "I'll make sure in our advertising that everyone is aware of the various alternatives besides a straight cash donation."

"I'm not sure if this is allowed, but is it possible to go on a brief tour today?" Jake asked, putting the dog down to visit with Charlie. Admittedly, he was reluctant to leave a place filled with good memories. "Only if it's convenient. I can come back at another time, if you want."

"It's no trouble at all. I'm tied up," Jill said. "And my husband Don is off looking at a horse who needs rescuing. But Cassie could take you around. She knows the way better than anyone. That is, if she's free."

"I would love to," Cassie said. "C'mon, Charlie. Let's show Jake around."

"Would you mind if I brought Gladys along for a walk?" he asked.

"Not at all," Jill said. "She'll love the exercise and mostly being with you."

She handed him a leash, which he clipped on. Gladys was so excited, she practically raced out the door.

"Whoa, girl," Jake said, laughing at how happy she was. Charlie ran up beside her as if showing her she needed to slow it down, and the two of them walked in front, side by side.

"Charlie's the perfect trainer," Jake said.

"Well, he certainly seems to love being around Gladys," Cassie said, as they all trekked over to the next barn where she opened the door. "This is where most of the horses are."

Cassie greeted each one by name as she led them down the middle, where they could see all the stalls. The dogs were oblivious to anything but themselves, so they dropped the leashes and let them be.

"You obviously come here a lot," he said, flicking his head back and forth, watching the horses as well as her enraptured face.

"I do. Almost every week. But look here, I have a surprise for you." She took his hand, which he had to admit he liked way too much and led him to the last stall.

Glancing at the name posted above the entryway, his mouth fell open.

"Are you kidding me?" he gasped. "Clyde is still here?"

"Sure is. The oldest horse on the farm and he's still thriving."

As if in response, Clyde shook his head and let out a loud whinny. "I know he's mocking me," Jake said. "He remembers me sliding off him. I'm sure of it." Clyde moved closer, lowering his head as Jake reached out to pat him.

"He should." Cassie shook with laughter. "It was a momentous moment."

"It's great to see him. You know, I'd love to come back for a ride."

"That's a good idea." She grinned. "Maybe I should join you. To help you out of the mud again if you fall. I'll bring lots of paper towels."

"Very funny." But it made him smile. Once again, he felt they were right back to being ten years old and best friends. "But I'd like that. At least there's no mud in the winter."

"Good point. Okay, it's a plan."

Picking up the leashes again, they left the barn and walked back to the car.

"Just a moment," Jake said. "I have to take Gladys in, and there's something I need to talk to Jill about. I'll be back in a few seconds."

He hurried to the office.

Nine

Jake wanted to talk to Jill about something?

And he sounded secretive?

Cassie figured he must be booking a riding lesson. He was genuinely excited to be out at the farm and seemed eager to get back on Clyde.

A flash of guilt sliced through her. Spending time with Jake showed her how much she missed him, but it also drilled home how rude she'd been when they'd first reconnected. He'd been nice, and she'd been cool.

"C'mon, Charlie, let's remind him that we'll come too. He might have thought I was just being polite and didn't mean it."

As they walked to the office, movement caught her eye and she glanced in the window. Surprisingly, she saw Jill hugging Jake tightly with one hand, while brushing away tears with the other.

"Oops. Looks like a private moment." She backed away fast. "C'mon, boy. Guess I should have considered this, since he didn't invite us."

Cassie hurried to the car, secured Charlie in the back, and got into the driver's seat to wait.

Seeing Jill cry disturbed her.

She was one of the strongest people Cassie'd ever met and she hoped Jill's tears were of joy, not sadness. Maybe she was just happy Gladys had taken a liking to Jake. It was always exciting to see our pets really take to someone.

Jake.

He still had that beautiful smile she'd thought about over the years and those mischievous blue eyes. She was amazed he was back in her life, even briefly. Seeing him again reminded her of all the fun times they'd had together, but it broke her heart to hear how down he'd been years ago. Wow. Homeless and living in a camper. Closing her eyes, she wondered why. What broke that happy, sweet ten-year-old she once knew, who was caring and kind to everyone? She didn't feel comfortable asking—after all, they hadn't been in each other's lives in years, but she hoped that maybe he'd tell her one day. And she could somehow offer support.

Charlie barked, and her eyes popped open. He was signaling Jake was back.

"Sorry I took so long," he said, settling his long legs in the passenger's seat. He reached in and pulled out something from a large bag he was carrying. "I spotted the farm baseball caps before you took me on the tour and wanted to get one. Hope you don't mind, but I suggested to Jill that it'd be a good idea if all the volunteers wore these caps with the horse logo on it at the fundraiser. She liked the idea, so I got a bunch." He popped one on his head and handed her another. They were navy blue highlighting their logo – a golden horse with the words Joyful Second Chances stamped on it. She slipped it on while Jake leaned over and put the bag in the back.

"Thanks, I've been meaning to get one," Cassie said. "And what a terrific idea. This way folks will know who to go to with their questions." *Did that cause Jill to cry?* "Did you pay for them? I can reimburse the expense."

"Oh, no problem." He grinned. "My treat. Jill was donating them, but I insisted on paying for them. I figure any amount of money will help with this terrific farm."

"That's kind of you."

"Well, this farm is incredible, and Jill is as wonderful as I remember her. I haven't met Don yet, but I really admire all the good work they do."

"Me, too."

She started the car and pulled out.

"You seem at home here," he said softly.

"Well, I really look at it as my second home. I love coming out here and pitching in. Helping those horses live a happier, enriching life is cathartic."

"I understand. I would join you if I still lived here."

"That would have been nice. Gladys really took to you. Have you ever had a dog?"

"No, but that little beagle is adorable. By the way, Jill mentioned the town Christmas tree light-up night. Is it tonight? I remember seeing it on a list Holly left me, but never checked the date."

"Yes, it is, as a matter of fact."

She noticed he never mentioned why Jill was upset. Should she ask? No, better not. Then she'd have to explain why she was looking in the window. Best to leave it alone.

"I only went once, but I remember it well," Jake said. "It's when they light up the giant Christmas tree along the river, as well as the gazebo, and the various decorations around the park, right?"

"That's correct." Cassie nodded.

"And there was free hot chocolate and popcorn and all sorts of goodies." He laughed. "I can recall having a stomach ache from all the stuff I ate that night." He glanced at her. "I think I saw it with you back when we were ten."

He remembered. She wondered if he recalled taking her hand that night and pulling her through the crowd so they could stand in the front row. They even kept on holding hands, and from that moment on, everyone began teasing them, saying they were madly in love with each other. Looking back, she figured they might not have been wrong. He had meant a lot to her as a kid. Definitely her first big crush.

Oops. Better answer him.

"Yes, we saw it together. I'm going." Should she ask him? Oh, why not. "Would you like to join me?"

Cassie hoped he'd say yes. She was enjoying his company even though still mad at him for leaving her all those years ago without a goodbye. She'd have to ask him about that one day if they continued to stay in touch.

"I'd like that."

She breathed a sigh of relief.

"Maybe I'll run into the woman who helped me and recognize her," he added. "It just dawned on me that the dog would be much older now."

Now that disappointed her. Was that the only reason he wanted to go?

"What kind of dog was it?"

"I don't know. I didn't get a clear look."

She pulled into the bed and breakfast, sad the drive was over. Mostly, it was lighthearted and fun, just the way it used to be.

"How about I meet you at the gazebo around six thirty?" she asked.

"I'll be there." He leaned back to pat Charlie on the head and left.

After dropping him off, Cassie drove back to her apartment to grab a bite to eat. She still couldn't get Jill's tears off her mind. She couldn't recall ever seeing her cry and considered calling her, but then would have to admit she had seen them through the window.

She pulled to a stop outside her apartment building. “Come on, Charlie. Let’s get something to eat before we head out again.”

She had only been in her home for a few minutes, just in time to pet Panda who had greeted her, purring, when the phone rang.

It was Jill.

It was almost as if she knew Cassie was thinking of her.

“Hi there,” Cassie said.

“Hello. Just wanted to thank you again for all the fundraising you’re doing. I appreciate it a lot.”

“No problem.” Cassie laughed. “I think you thank me every time you see me. You don’t have to, you know. What you do means a lot to me. How you take care of all those beautiful horses and teach as well is beyond me.”

“Guess I just love what I do. Er, did Jake tell you what he did?”

“Sure. He bought baseball caps for everyone to wear. I think it’s an excellent idea to have the volunteers stand out to assist and help.”

“Yes, he did do that, but did he tell you he donated ten thousand dollars?”

“What?” Cassie plopped down on the couch. No wonder Jill had cried. They were indeed tears of joy.

“Can you believe it? What an incredibly kind person he is.”

“He sure is.” And always was. She remembered the time a little boy in the first grade fell during recess and Jake rushed over to help him up. He even pulled a lollipop out of his pocket and handed it to the little guy, who sat on a bench for the rest of the break eating it, grinning from ear to ear.

“Er, I wanted to ask you. Please jog my memory. Is he the boy who fell off Clyde years ago?” Jill asked. “In the mud?”

“Yes. That’s him.” She couldn’t help but giggle.

“I hear you laughing.” Jill let out a roar as well. “He mentioned coming out for a ride. I’ll have to give him a calmer horse. I was just glad he didn’t get hurt when he fell.”

“Oh, I’m sure he’ll want Clyde again. To prove something.”

“He also mentioned he was searching for a woman who ‘rainbowed’ him years ago.” Jill’s voice took on a serious note.

“Yes, he is. I wish he’d leave that alone. If she’s doing it anonymously, she doesn’t want to be known.”

“I agree. Ahhh—is there anything going on between you two?”

What?

“Oh no, nothing.”

“You sure? I saw sparks.”

“No sparks. None whatsoever.”

“All right. If you say so.”

Cassie knew she was lying. She acknowledged, at least to herself, that there were a few sparks. Even fireworks. It seemed her crush had lasted all these years and even beyond the hurt she’d felt. But she didn’t feel comfortable talking about it. At least, not yet. Anyway, he’d be leaving soon and that would be it. The end.

They chatted for a few more minutes, then disconnected. After all, they’d be seeing each other at the light up night shortly.

“Well, Charlie and Panda, I didn’t forget about you. Let’s get some supper before the big night starts.”

She gave them both their dinners and after soup and salad, Cassie bundled up since it was expected to turn cold. “Hey, Panda. You keep an eye on the apartment. C’mon, boy, time to see the pretty lights.”

She laughed as Panda curled up on the couch, looking the picture of peace and contentment. She’d probably move to the bedroom and her pillow shortly. Or my pillow, that is. Cassie took a moment to watch her stretch, groom herself, then close her eyes. Sometimes she envied her cat’s life of sleeping, eating, and cuddling. Her continuous purring showed how happy she was not getting involved in the drama that sometimes overtook their lives. She was a constant reminder to enjoy life more.

"Sleep well, little one." Cassie patted her on the head then continued to get ready for Rainbow's big night – the beginning of Christmas celebrations.

"Here, Charlie. Let's get your coat on, too."

After bundling him up, they headed out on the short walk to the gazebo along the river. As they drew nearer, she took a moment to soak it all in.

It was one of her favorite nights of the year.

The whole town gathered to share in the joy of the Christmas season. She'd been coming with her parents since a wee baby and really missed them tonight. Looking around, she smiled at the laughter she witnessed and sucked in wisps of hot chocolate and popcorn. Jake wasn't the only one who had stuffed himself with the free food being offered. Speaking of Jake, she saw him approaching, weaving in and out of the crowd, this time wearing a toque, scarf, and gloves.

"Hi there," he said. He handed her a hot chocolate, and there was that smile of his again. To her surprise, her heart sped up and she felt breathless.

Guess the cold was getting to her.

Surely, she wasn't reacting to his nearness. Or was she?

According to romance novels, she probably was, but it was a new feeling for her.

Ignore it.

There was no future here. Not when they lived in different provinces, let alone towns.

"Thanks. Glad to see you bundled up. It's cold tonight," she said quickly, trying to distract her thoughts.

"It is, but nice and fresh at the same time." He reached down to give Charlie a pat on the head. "It's pretty special that practically the whole town comes out. Now if only we had a touch of snow, it would be perfect." As if cued on a movie set, large fluffy snowflakes started falling. "I see I have power." He stood up, laughing. She joined in and was surprised when he took her hand and led her closer to the front of the gazebo. Exactly as he'd done all those years ago.

"Hey, Ms. Blackwood." She glanced over to see a group of her students approaching, Lainey in the lead. Oh, oh. She noted their glances at their hands, and she was sure there would be questions later in class. They were always trying to set her up with a single uncle or a friend of their parents. Anyone, really.

"Hi there," she said, subtly yanking her hand away. They looked curiously at Jake. "This is Jake Williams who also attended our school when he was in grade five. He's helping with the fundraiser as well."

"Great," said Lainey. "Will he be there when we set up tomorrow?"

"Do you need help?" Jake asked.

"Sure do," the girl said.

"Well, count me in then."

"Only if you're free," Cassie said, wanting him to come, yet wishing he wouldn't. She was starting to like having him around way too much. "And this is Lainey, the one who came up with the idea of the fundraiser."

"Well, pleased to meet you, Lainey." He reached out and shook her hand. Cassie noticed her student's eyes were beaming.

"And I am free, and I'd be glad to help you tomorrow," he continued.

"Good," Lainey said, as she introduced him to the others. Judging by their smiles, he seemed to be charming each one of them, Cassie thought. She'd forgotten his powerful effect on others. When they were kids, everyone gravitated to him, wanting to hang around with him. She always felt special that she was the closest to him and he always picked her to sit with and walk home with after school.

"Excuse me. May I have everyone's attention?" The words shouted out through a speaker system, and they all looked at the gazebo as the mayor continued, "We'll begin the night as per tradition with a few Christmas carols sung by the Rainbow school choir."

This was another tradition that always warmed Cassie's heart. Joy flooded her as children sang out with their sweet voices and adults joined in. After rocking renditions of "Frosty the Snowman," "Jingle Bells," and "Deck the Halls," the mayor invited everyone to join him in the final countdown.

"One, two, three"—anticipation spread through the crowd—and as they all hit 'ten' the twenty foot Christmas tree standing before them exploded in light. It was absolutely breathtaking and never failed to stun her. Cassie looked around at the many images of reindeer, Santa, angels, and snowmen, which were all lit up next, and she literally started to shake from excitement.

Immediately Jake wrapped his arm around her.

"You're cold," he said.

Moved by his touch, and liking it too much, she wanted to pull away but somehow couldn't, students or not. She knew in that moment, the second one of the evening, she'd have to guard her heart even more, for she was in danger of falling for him all over again. She couldn't be hurt a second time. In grade five, she was a kid, but she couldn't go through that again. This time, as an adult, it would hurt even harder.

After saying goodbye, she hurried home with Charlie.

But she knew she'd treasure that moment forever.

Sigh.

But it was a good sigh.

A sigh of joy.

For even a brief moment in time, she had her best friend back.

Ten

I was seventeen when mom passed away.

Twelve years ago, today.

I was devastated.

As per tradition, here I sat, on my favorite bench, gazing at the sky. My fur friend snuggled beside me while I was deep in thought.

It had been a busy night.

Three baskets were delivered.

One filled with diapers to a struggling single mom, one with books and puzzles to a lonely senior with a link to a support group, and another with a small cash donation to someone with a sick pup, to help pay the costly veterinarian bills. My dog even got involved and picked out a candy cane stuffed toy to add to that gift.

Mom.

Sigh.

I had high hopes chemotherapy would give me more time with her.

It didn't.

My heart was broken the day she passed.

It was also the day I discovered her secret.

And what a secret it was.

A really big one.

My mom had a sacred place in the house. Most people would call it an office but she called it her sacred place. She even had a sign with that title hanging off the door. It was a small room off the kitchen, and missing her so much, I wandered in and sat on her chair, crying my eyes out. I kept hoping she'd appear at the door as if nothing had happened, hug me, and say, "How are you doing, my sweet girl?"

I loved being her sweet girl.

Wanting to feel her near me, I got up off the chair and walked around, running my hands over her things, when to my surprise I found twenty-five baskets on a shelf tucked away behind a mountain of pens, pencils, and paper. All were shades of pink, blue, green, yellow, and red. I also found a key hanging from a nail in the wall that opened a large cupboard in the corner of the room. In it, I had discovered all sorts of items – canned goods, Kleenex, jars of peanut butter, diapers – and a box of notes with rainbows on them and the words, 'You are loved' in her handwriting.

What?

That was odd.

As if I had stumbled into another universe or something. Another world.

I remembered racing to my father screaming, "Something weird is going on. Was Mom running a store or something? Did she have a secret life?"

He smiled, led me to the kitchen, and over cocoa and chocolate chip cookies, calmly said, "Guess it's time you know the truth. Have you ever heard of that expression around town, 'You have been rainbowed?'"

"I have," I said. "Everyone has. It's when you receive a gift anonymously. You have no idea who gave it to you."

"You're right."

Silence.

Then it hit me.

"The baskets? The cards? The food?" I had stood, shocked. "Are you trying to tell me Mom is the one who rainbowed people?"

"Yes," he whispered.

I had been stunned.

I still was.

I'd had no idea.

Imagine living with the rainbow giver and not knowing it.

I'd even remembered an article in the paper, one my mom had cut out and stored in a drawer, where a reporter sought the identity of this kind person. He asked for people to let him know who they thought it was. Even offered a cash reward if they picked the right person. Cassie remembered excited chatter as people guessed, but funny thing, there was no follow-up article with the answer.

It was still a secret, dad said, and I honored that.

I never told a soul.

Then and now.

Eleven

Jake stared at his computer. He'd written nothing in the past hour. Not one word.

His days in Rainbow were ticking by fast and he was no further ahead in figuring out who his mystery helper was. He smacked his fist on the desk in frustration.

I should have had more of a plan, he thought.

It wasn't like she was going to magically appear before him, but to be honest, he had figured it wouldn't be this hard. After all, this was a really small town where most people knew each other's business. You'd think someone would have dropped a hint by now.

Pushing his chair back, he stood and paced back and forth. Suddenly he clearly remembered something his mother had told him. "If you want to know what's going on, talk to the town librarian. They always know the pulse of what is happening locally."

She was right.

Jake had fond memories of being herded, along with his brother, into the car every Saturday morning for a trip to the local library. He used to love walking up and down the aisles searching through stacks of books, selecting ones that caught his eye. He was still an avid reader but hadn't been to a library in years. He should fix that. Now.

Off he went to the Rainbow Public Library.

It was preferable to just sitting in his room trying to conjure up a miracle. He wasn't convinced he would find any information about the concept of being rainbowed and who was behind it, but it was worth a try. He had several viable suspects: Cassie, Kelly, Holly, her mother, Anna. All were kind, interested in people, and he guessed would help in a pinch. He desperately needed to narrow down his list.

Cassie.

Just thinking of her made him smile as he recalled how happy she looked during light-up night. He remembered how much she loved that special event and while holding her hand briefly, with the twinkly lights, the smell of popcorn and chocolate wafting around them, he had felt joy for the first time in a long time. She had been special to him at ten years old, and obviously still was.

Stop it.

Cassie showed no indication whatsoever of wanting to get involved, but he was interested. It just felt right having her back in his life.

Forget it.

Back to the librarian. Maybe she knew some vital information.

Walking briskly, he reveled in the fact that in a small town, almost everything was within walking distance. The library was not far from his bed and breakfast, and was housed in a glorious old two-story red brick building that looked stunning, all dressed up for Christmas. Walking up the steps to the front door, he was especially impressed with the large wreath hanging there. As well as twinkling gold and silver lights, small photos of favorite Christmas stories were woven throughout the greenery. He could make out one of Rudolph and Frosty the Snowman and, of course, everyone's favorite, "'Twas the night before Christmas." A nice library touch which flooded him with memories of pleasant times spent there. He wondered if they still had those green and white mints wrapped in plastic sitting on the check-out desk. As a kid, he used to fill his pockets before leaving and chew on them all day long.

Opening the door, a "Welcome," greeted him. The friendly woman standing behind the large oak desk smiled. "Come on in."

"Hello there," he said, walking over. "Thanks for the warm greeting."

"Well, you're new here, or at least I haven't seen you before. I'm Ellen Aston." She reached out to shake his hand.

"Jake Williams. Actually, I lived here as a kid for about a year and I am very familiar with the library. Come to think of it, there was a woman back then with the same last name as yours."

"Oh, my aunt must have been here at the time. Tall, slim, short grey hair. Laura Aston was her name."

"That's her. Really nice lady." In fact, it was almost an exact description of herself, except she had black hair. "She used to sneak me chocolate chip cookies, but made me promise not to tell."

"Yes, that would be her." Ellen laughed. "She's a retired lady of leisure now."

He glanced down at the bowl. "Oh, and I remember those mints."

"Yes, they have been around forever. Oh, not the same mints." She laughed. "I fill the bowl every day. Some of the younger ones take handfuls."

"Guilty as charged." He smiled. "When I was a kid, of course."

"Well, feel free to indulge yourself. But may I help you with something else? Or are you just here for some books to read?"

"I have an odd request. I understand there is a kind person in town who, for years, has been doing good deeds on a regular basis. Have you heard the expression 'you've been rainbowed?'"

Ellen paused. Her eyes darted about and, like everyone else he'd asked, Jake was sure she knew.

"No, well, yes, I have heard of that expression. But my understanding is whoever it is wants their identity kept a secret. I've never delved into it. Why do you ask?"

"I've been 'rainbowed' myself and I'd love to thank the person who did it."

"Really?" She looked as interested as Kelly over at the restaurant.

"Yes."

"With colored baskets and cards that say, 'you are loved?'"

Seemed like everyone knew the details.

"Yes. Do you know who it is?"

She shook her head. "Sorry, I can't help you."

He felt she could, but was just not telling. It seemed to be some kind of townwide secret."

"Are you sure?" He explained that he didn't want to just thank the person, but also wanted to write an article to promote the good work she does, then added, "People should know about this kind of person. She should be recognized for her good work."

"You're a journalist, are you?"

"Yes."

"Well, that's even more reason not to tell. Even if I knew, which I don't. But if they choose to remain quiet and keep their identity unknown, they will not want it to appear in a newspaper."

"Maybe. Maybe not. You have absolutely no information at all about the 'rainbow' giver?"

A thought hit him. What if it was her aunt? She was certainly the kindest librarian he had ever met. Maybe Ellen was just covering for her.

"Well. I would be remiss not to tell you that years ago someone wrote about this in the local paper. You could check it out. I remember it well because from time-to-time people bring up being rainbowed and are curious over who is doing this. The old papers are not online, but we have copies on microfilm. The story was in the December issue, about twenty years ago." She typed away at her computer. "December fourteenth, to be exact. I kept track of the date to have it handy, just in case."

"Just the one article?"

"Yes. No follow up."

"And twenty years ago? It's been going on that long?"

"Yes, maybe longer. Here, follow me." She led him over to the microfilm projectors and found the article for him. "There you go."

"Thank you."

"No problem. Let me know if you have any further questions. I have to run. I have a class coming in and some preparation to do yet."

"Thanks, I will."

Twenty years ago. Hmmm. The woman he saw seemed about twenty. Her voice sounded youthful, and the way she moved suggested a younger person. This would make the woman he was seeking around forty. Maybe older. Good to know. It definitely eliminated Cassie. And Holly. But it narrowed it down a little.

Reading the news item, he noted it was written by a James Passel, who expressed wonder over who had done these incredibly generous actions. He then attempted what Jake was doing—tried to find out who performed these acts of kindnesses and even put out an appeal for people to contact him if they knew. He either had no luck or someone spoke to him about it because, as Ellen said, there was no follow-up article with his findings.

Strange. Normally a reporter would let his readers know the results of his research. Not Mr. Passel. For some reason, he just dropped it.

He leaned back in his chair. Hmm. So he wasn't the only one who had tried to track down the rainbow lady.

Glancing over, he noticed the librarian was free and hurried over.

"Do you know James Passel? The man who wrote the article?"

"Yes, I do."

"Is he still here working as a reporter?"

"Certainly. The newspaper office is just down the street. Take a right at Clarence and you'll see it."

"Well, thank you for your help."

"No problem. Come back anytime." She picked up a handful of mints and handed them to him. "For old times' sake."

Laughing, he immediately stuffed them in his pocket, just as he'd done as a kid.

"Thanks," he said, "for all your help and for the mints."

"No problem." She paused. "I'd leave it alone though, if I were you."

"Pardon?" Jake was caught by surprise. One minute Ellen Aston was all smiley and friendly and handing him mints, the next she was frowning and put a whole new spin on the words, 'if looks could kill.'

"You heard me."

She turned her back on him and walked into a room behind the desk.

Twelve

So much for Ms. Aston's kind words of 'Come back anytime.'

Jake didn't think he'd be welcomed again anytime soon. He wondered what that was all about. It seemed the subject of 'rainbowing' was a touchy one, which made him want to delve into it even more. There was a story there. He felt it deep in his gut and he was going to keep on digging.

Walking out of the library, he unrolled a mint and popped it into his mouth. He was immediately transformed into that little kid who spent many an afternoon in the library curled up with a book. They were good times, he thought, when the written word opened whole new worlds to him. He had to get back to reading even more and not being on the go as much.

Arriving at a side street, he glanced up at the sign. Clarence Street. Turning right, he immediately spotted the newspaper building. Ellen was right. You couldn't miss it. It was a large white wooden building, with the name *Rainbow News*, splashed across it in bright red paint. Surprisingly, it was sparsely decorated with just one straggly wreath on the door in the token Christmas color scheme. It gave across a 'bah, humbug' kind of feeling amid all the other buildings and homes covered in bright lights with decorations screaming, "Christmas is here!" Could be the reason was the large for sale sign on the lawn. That was interesting. Was the newspaper going out of business? Or just moving to another building? He noticed there was a yellow-colored machine off to the side where you could insert coins to get a copy of the paper. He hadn't seen one of those in a while, but he quickly dug out a few coins and purchased one. Flicking through it fast, he was impressed. It was newsy, interesting, and covered everything locally – sports, events, occasions. And it all seemed to be handled by one reporter. Passel. Time to find him.

Opening the door, he walked in. Seeing no one, he said loudly, "Excuse me. I'm looking for a Mr. James Passel."

"Yes. Over here."

A tall, lean, elderly man pushed back his chair, stood, and came towards Jake, hand outstretched. He had been hidden behind a stack of books perched on a desk in the corner.

"I've seen you around. How can I help you?" he asked.

"Thank you." Jake shook his hand. "The name's Jake. I was at the library and read an article you wrote years ago about being 'rainbowed.'"

"Grab a seat." James pointed to a small sitting area in the corner. Jake noticed he was limping and seemed to have trouble walking. After they sat, he said, "I remember that story well."

"But I noticed you didn't do a follow-up."

He shook his head. "No, I didn't."

"May I ask why?"

He shrugged. "Just never felt the need to."

Jake felt James' nonchalance was a cover. He probably knew more, just wasn't going to get into it. Just like everyone else.

"Did you ever figure out who was doing it?"

"No. Never did."

Of course, Jake didn't believe him. He was probably protecting her identity for some reason.

"Well, it's unbelievable this person can do a lot of good, and no one knows who it is." He decided to keep digging. Surely, he'd find a clue somewhere, or someone would slip up at some point.

"They're good at leaving a basket and sneaking away fast, I guess." James stared at him, curiosity evident in his eyes. "Why do you care?"

"I was 'rainbowed' myself five years ago. I wanted to thank the person who did it." He hesitated, then said, "And it was a woman."

"Really?" He sat straight up. "And you never saw her face?"

"No. Wish I had."

"Kelly said you're a newspaper reporter."

"Yes, I am." Aha. He must eat at the diner. Guess a new person in town was of interest, especially to another reporter.

"And you plan to write an article about this?" His eyes continued to hold Jake's.

"Yes. When I find out who is behind it all."

"I see." He shook his head fast. "That's a big mistake."

Same old, same old. Jake also wondered if the librarian had called and warned him.

"But you tried once."

He nodded. "I did, but got nowhere."

"Are you sure?"

"I'm sure."

Jake rolled his eyes in frustration. He just couldn't help it. "I don't see what the big deal is in uncovering the rainbow giver. She's doing good work and I just want to thank her. She deserves to be recognized for her kindness."

"Not if she doesn't want to be."

"And you know this for sure?"

Jake watched him closely. "No, I don't. As I said, I never found out who it was."

Jake didn't believe that one bit, but figured he wasn't going to get any more information out of him. "I see you're selling the building," he asked. "Is the paper closing or are you just moving?"

"It's closing. I'm retiring. I'm getting too old to run around collecting stories." He pointed to a cane leaning against the side of his desk. "I fell a few years back and my knees have never been the same."

"I'm sorry to hear that. There will be no paper in Rainbow at all after you leave?"

"No. Or at least no one has shown any interest. Folks here mostly read the larger city one, anyway. They cover our town, too. I doubt anyone will miss it."

"Oh, I think they will. You do a good, thorough job." He held up the paper sitting on his lap. "And you have a nice writing style. Easy to read and easy to understand."

James raised his eyebrows. "Well, thank you."

"I mean it. You're a good writer."

James seemed to perk up after that and they small talked for a while. Jake hadn't complimented him to get something out of him, but it was interesting hearing James talk about his job and the town. It was obvious he loved it here.

"I'm surprised no one wants to carry this on," Jake said.

"Well, I never married, I also have no family interested and most reporters would rather write for a bigger production." He scratched his head and shrugged. "Can't say I blame them. It's more money and they're not a one-person show. They have more help. Here, you do it all. Reporting, printing, selling, advertising, delivering. I have only one other employee, who has taken a job in Ottawa. He'll be leaving soon."

"Well, I really enjoy working for a small-town newspaper. I love the community atmosphere and really getting to know the townsfolk."

"I agree with you there. I've enjoyed working here too."

"Sounds like you don't really want to leave."

"I don't, but I have no choice. It's too much for me now."

"Are you staying around?"

"Of course." He nodded vigorously. "Rainbow is a great place to live."

"I see that. I lived here for a year as a kid and remember the town well." He noticed James check his watch and his eyes kept darting to his phone, indicating he was probably busy. Or expecting someone. Jake stood. "Well, thank you for the chat. I've taken up too much of your time as is. I've missed this town and now I know why. Everyone is friendly and kind."

"Yes, they are."

Jake shook his hand and left, planning to go back at some point to chat with James again. Oh, not about his mystery woman—he figured that was a dead end, but he enjoyed hearing Passel's views on the town from a reporter's perspective.

His mystery woman.

Sigh.

Jake had figured it would be hard to find her, but not impossible. Now, it was looking like he'd made this trip for nothing. Well, not really, since he had connected again with Cassie and he liked that. A lot. Too much, actually.

Guess no one wanted him to find the 'rainbow' giver. But surely someone would give it away at some point.

He was counting on it.

It was just a matter of time.

And then he'd write his article...

Thirteen

Oh, no!

I can't believe it.

Someone is trying to expose the identity of the rainbow giver.

Me.

They're trying to expose me!

And they are planning on writing a story.

Once again.

About me.

I hugged my dog even tighter.

No way could I allow that.

It would ruin everything.

The whole premise of what my mother was trying to do.

My mom.

I sat back on the park bench thinking of her.

She was incredibly kind.

Every Christmas, she volunteered at a dinner for those who were in need, or maybe just all alone and wanted company. My dad and I joined her, and I would never forget the beautiful guests' smiles and the way they went out of the way to thank us for being there for them. Mom used to remind us that yes, we were giving, but they were giving right on back. They had touched my heart in many ways with their joy and their stories. They all had tales to tell that fascinated me, and I saw Mom made a point of thanking each one of them for coming. We were all equal, she said, just at different stages of our lives.

I had heard many times at school how people had been moved to tears by the kindness of a basketful of goodies. My mother had literally saved lives in numerous ways. She was always reaching out to others, and one of her favorite sayings was, "If you are ever feeling down, do something for someone else, and you'll feel much better."

She was right.

I wiped a tear drifting down.

I always knew how compassionate she was, but to discover she was the rainbow giver still blew me away.

My heart burst with pride, knowing it was my mom who had orchestrated all of that.

And then came her funeral.

The day that changed my life.

Heartbroken, I had listened to the kind words people said about my mom at the funeral home, and later at the church. I heard many stories of how she fed them, took care of their children, and was the first person to call if times were tough.

Wow! If they only knew what she did in private with no witnesses.

Inspired and overflowing with love, before the funeral was even finished, I made a decision.

As a matter of fact, I could remember the exact moment I decided to continue my mother's legacy of kindness.

It was when Mary Beth Simmons spoke about how Mom called her mother every single day when she was recovering from a broken leg. Apparently, Mom became her cheerleader and helped her recover not just from the broken limb, but also from depression, as she looked more positively on life.

Mary Beth went on and on about how my mom had made a difference.

I had sat straight up in the church pew.

Her words hit me hard.

I wanted to make a difference in people's lives, too.

I wanted to 'rainbow' people.

I wanted to continue all the good work my mom did.

Instead of crying and feeling sorry for myself, I was going to move forward and help others.

Anonymously.

This was what my mother would have wanted.

I never told my dad, but I was sure he knew.

As a teen, I used to sneak out at all hours of the day and night to deliver goodies, and made up a million excuses about where I was.

No one had discovered what I did.

But I sure didn't want anyone snooping around.

Taking a deep breath in, I counted to ten as I let it out to calm down.

No way would I allow my identity to be discovered. In revealing mine, it revealed my mother's.

It was to be kept a secret.

Staring up at the heavens, I whispered to the stars, "Don't worry, Mom. It won't happen. No one will find out."

I also sent up a prayer for the two baskets I had given out today. One to a woman who had just lost her mother and another to a man whose business had crumbled.

"In your memory, Mom, as always," I said louder, as my dog licked my face in solidarity. "This time, like every time, is for you."

Oh, how I missed her.

Fourteen

"How's the article coming along?" Evan asked.

Jake eyed his computer screen. It was blank. Again. The glare off it blinded him for a second.

"I'm making progress." Better not let him know he had nothing. His brother didn't need more stress in his life.

"Great. Looking forward to reading it."

Me, too, Jake thought.

They chatted for a while, ended the call, and he got back to writing or at least attempting to put some words together under a title. Typing on his laptop, he wrote, 'Rainbowed.' Under this heading he added a few sentences about his past, then...*Meet the woman behind the saying, 'you have been rainbowed.' Today I discovered who my mystery giver is...'*

Yeah, right.

Even after a visit to the library and the local newspaper, he'd failed to come up with the slightest clue who she was. He discovered 'rainbowing' people was a pattern with her, and possibly a town guarded secret, but he had to be open to the fact he may never find out her identity.

Wait, was that a knock at the door?

He hurried to open it, glad of even the slightest interruption.

"I noticed you didn't go out for breakfast," Holly said, handing him a tray holding a coffee, a plate of bacon and eggs, cutlery, napkins, and various condiments. "I brought you something to eat. I remember you mentioning this was your favorite breakfast."

His stomach rumbled at the sight and smell. "Why, thank you. I got up early to write and forgot to head to the café. This is incredibly kind of you. It definitely is my favorite."

"No problem. I figure you're busy." She grinned, also handing over a bag. "Brought you some cookies too. Gingerbread and shortbread. Enjoy and have a good day."

"Thanks. You, too." As she turned to leave, he said, "Hey, Holly."

"Yes?"

"I was just wondering if you have heard of the expression being 'rainbowed'?"

She hesitated for a second, then said, "Yes, a few times."

His heart beat fast. "Do you know who is doing it?"

"Um, no. I can't help you there. Sorry."

But her eyes were downcast, and Jake was sure she knew or suspected, like everyone else he had talked to.

"Well, okay then."

"Why are you trying to find this person?" She looked up. "Is it important?"

"To me. I was 'rainbowed' once."

"Really?"

"Yes. This person saved my life and I want to thank her."

"You know it was a woman?"

He detected the interest in her eyes, similar to Kelly's.

"Yes. I saw her and her dog. Not clearly, though."

"You can't really describe her?"

"No. She had a hat and scarf, and the dog was black but I have no idea what breed."

"Is that why you wanted to know if I had a dog?"

"You got me." Jake could feel his face turn red, realizing he'd been that transparent.

"But what if she doesn't want you to know?"

Once again, it seemed like everyone said the same thing. It was as if he were cast in a movie or something, and everyone had the same script for what to say when asked about 'rainbowing.' Holly sounded annoyed, though. Really annoyed.

"Why wouldn't she? People enjoy being thanked."

"Not everyone."

Was she speaking from experience?

"Well, I think she deserves to be thanked."

"I doubt she'd agree, providing it really is a woman. Anyhow, enjoy your breakfast." She took off fast, before he had a chance to say anything more, effectively shutting down their conversation. Once again, the same script. Warn him off, and then leave, or change the topic.

Practically inhaling the food, all Jake could think of was, *Why did all the townsfolk he'd talked to go out of their way to be evasive?* No wonder he was having a hard time finding his helper. It could be anyone and no one was talking. Although he'd ruled out Holly, figuring she was too young, he was sure she knew who it was.

Or, maybe not.

Once again it hit him that maybe no one really knew. Could be they suspected but had discovered the woman didn't want to be acknowledged. Maybe they didn't want to know. Maybe they liked the fantasy of a mysterious rainbow giver jumping in to help. Like a superhero.

His brother's worried eyes rose before him. More than ever, Jake figured his search might be fruitless, but he was going to keep on trying. He couldn't give up. He couldn't lose sight of his goal. He had to help Evan.

Swigging down the coffee, he glanced at the clock: seven a.m. Well, at least he had managed to put a few words on the screen. A bit of an introduction. Now, to keep doing research. When all else failed, start from scratch. He began googling for any information about Rainbow. He had already searched for 'rainbow giver' and come up with nothing. Now he was looking to see if anything was mentioned on the town sites or articles. To his shock, he discovered they had their own Facebook page. He should have thought of that before. Most towns these days had a special page to highlight events, local businesses, needs, and wants.

He joined and was quickly accepted.

Scouring it, he looked for any mention of being 'rainbowed' and after a search, eventually found one reference. A mother expressed joy at receiving a red basket of diapers when she was at the end of her rope financially. But of course, there was no mention of who could have possibly done that. She did say she had received a bracelet with the words 'you are loved on it.' He fingered his. Looked like this was one of the rainbow giver's trademarks. Another interesting point was this particular act of kindness had taken place in the summer. The rainbow lady obviously didn't just stick to Christmas. Looked like she did this all year round. Whoever it was, really was an incredibly kind person.

He contemplated trying to look up this mother but was worried again he'd be giving away what he was searching for, and people might clam up even more than they already had. He was trying to ask only selected people, but now Cassie, the waitress, librarian, and reporter, knew. And Holly. It would spread across the town fast; he was sure of it. Better not bother that mother and create even more of a stir.

He continued exploring the internet, searching for anything else, but came up blank.

Glancing at his watch he saw it was close to lunchtime and he had promised to help set up the fundraiser at the school. He headed to the restaurant for more sustenance and then off to help Cassie. He was looking forward to seeing her again. Guess his crush had never really left him, since he felt himself wanting to be around her all the time. But he knew he had to back off. It was pointless. Odd how that thought bothered him. After all, he liked his new place in Manitoba, as well as his job. He'd have to get better at not thinking of her. When he left, they'd probably have no contact again.

That thought hit him hard. He didn't like it one bit. But it was his reality and he had to accept it.

Bundling up, he walked over to the restaurant. As soon as he walked in, Kelly approached him.

"I didn't see you at breakfast," she said. "I thought you might have left without saying goodbye again."

He smiled. It was nice to know someone cared. Or even noticed.

"I was just bogged down doing some work. What do you recommend for lunch?"

"Shepherd's Pie is the special today. And it's really good."

"Great. That's what I'll have."

Kelly had it there in two minutes. "By the way, have you found the identity of your rainbow basket giver yet?" Her furled eyebrows suggested she looked more worried than just interested.

"Not a clue."

"Good." She grinned.

He smiled. "It's comforting to know you are rooting for me to fail."

"You are best to leave things untouched." She turned and left.

He couldn't help but chuckle. At least he had discovered the way to get rid of people if he didn't feel like chatting. All he had to do was mention the 'rainbow' giver.

But he still disagreed.

Lots of people professed to be humble, but deep down, longed to be acknowledged. Or that was what he believed. His mystery lady deserved to be thanked for all the good she did. Too bad others didn't feel the same.

Forget about it.

Right now, he had some volunteering to do.

Practically scarfing down the pie, he paid his bill, left a tip, and hurried to the school.

Fifteen

Rainbow Elementary.

He stared up at the sign.

The words were in green and white, their school colors, and below it was a space to advertise events. Joyfest Fundraiser was written there with the date and time of its opening.

Excitement raced through him, for he had loved the year he'd attended there, and had assumed he'd be graduating from this very building.

Opening the main door, memories surfaced as he walked into the foyer. Immediately, he noticed how narrow the halls were. As a kid, he thought the school was huge, when in fact, it obviously wasn't. He saw his locker, remembering how excited he was to get it. At that time, only students in grade five and up got one and every time he opened it, he'd felt like such a big boy. Peeking in the window of his once-upon-a-time classroom, he noticed it was now a bright shade of blue where it had been painted green. He saw the pencil sharpener still attached to the windowsill, and what looked like the exact same clock, advertising the Sanctuary Nook on it hung on the wall. He could see feeders outside the windows, probably newer ones, but he remembered watching the various birds stop there and, of course, the many squirrels who managed to hang on enough to get seeds. Moving on to the gymnasium, he stepped inside and immediately closed his eyes, summoning up multiple sessions of basketball, volleyball, the smell of sweat, and the cheap cologne he used to slap on. Those were good times. And of course, they were also filled with Cassie's friendship. Her smiles, her kindness, meant the world to him. In fact, she was his whole world back then.

"Are you okay?"

His eyes popped open.

There was Cassie, baseball cap on, golden curls cascading, a concerned look on her face. A look he'd seen a million times back in grade five.

"Yes. Getting all nostalgic, I guess."

"I can see that, but yes. We had lots of fun times back then."

She felt it too? Could it be possible she had missed him as well? After all, she offered to go horseback riding with him.

Once again, forget it. Remember, you won't be in Rainbow much longer.

He looked around. "You have a lot of energetic volunteers here to help. Amazing, since it's the day before Christmas Eve day, and usually people are still running around getting last-minute gifts."

"It's remarkable. A real miracle, actually. My students got their parents, aunts, uncles, friends, and anyone free to lend a hand. Besides saving horses, Jill is a really popular teacher here." She smiled, excitement radiating from her. "Everyone wants to help."

"I can see that."

"But hey, thank you for coming." She handed him another cap. "I see you forgot yours. Ready for work?"

"You got it. What can I do?" He put the cap on and grinned. "Oh, by the way, I sold mine to an interested man staying at the bed and breakfast. I'll add the money to the donation box tomorrow."

"Oh, that's good to know. A sale already." Cassie winked as she called Lainey. "She's got the day all figured out," she said proudly. "Where would you like to put Jake to work?"

Lainey bobbed up and down, moving her feet back and forth, obviously extremely excited as she consulted her notebook. "Would you mind setting up tables?" She pointed to a group of students pulling out tables and chairs from under the stage. "I think they need some help."

"Certainly. I'll get right to work." He paused. "Wait a second. Cassie, is that Charlie I see in a crate over there?"

"Yes. It's too long to leave a pup. I figured he'd be safe there."

"I can take him out from time to time, if you'd like. I know you're going to be really busy."

"I would like that. Thank you."

The door opened and Jill walked in with a man who was probably Don. A joyful bark sounded out, and Jake laughed as Gladys jerked her leash out of Jill's hand and ran right to him.

"Hi there, girl." The little pup was beside herself, tail wagging so hard she kept falling over. He scooped her up in his arms.

"Can't get over how much she has taken to you," Jill said. "At home she's quite subdued."

"Well, it's mutual," Jake said.

"Oh, and this is Don," Jill said.

"Hello there." Jake held the pup under one arm as he reached out to shake his hand. Don had white hair, a white beard, was stocky and, yes, he resembled Santa Claus. He also had a big grin on his face and sparkly eyes, emanating a friendly warmth.

"Looks like you have a fan." He laughed as Gladys kept licking Jake's face. "I brought her crate as well." He walked over and put it beside Charlie's.

"I'm planning on taking Charlie out from time to time, could I bring Gladys too?" Jake asked.

"I think you have no choice," Jill said. "She will definitely want to go with you."

After Gladys was snoozing in her crate, Jake got to work, constantly sneaking glances at Cassie, admiring her warmth and kindness. It was obvious her students adored her by their lit-up faces whenever she was near. He also enjoyed hearing her laughter, which bounced around the room as she encouraged people, thanked them, and showed them where to put things.

I have got to stop thinking about her. She is too much of a distraction.

Fortunately, after setting up tables, he got busy helping Holly and her mother put together their booth. He looked at their sign. "Cozy Cookies," he said. "I know this will sellout. It's guaranteed."

"I hope," Holly said. "I've been riding at the farm for a while now and this is my way of paying back."

The door opened and in walked Kelly, holding several bags.

He rushed over. "Need some help?"

"Yes, thanks. I sure do."

She directed him to a corner where the sign said, "Coffee and pie."

"What a great idea!" he said.

"Anything to help."

"I've got the tablecloths," Cassie said, walking over holding a large box. "The school said we could use their Christmas ones."

"Great," Anna said. "Let's get these tables covered."

"I'll help too," Jake added.

They went from table to table covering them with festive cloths covered in Santas, reindeer and snowmen. Once again, he couldn't stop staring at Cassie and a few times she caught him, raising her eyebrows. As a grown man, he found himself back to being ten again, enjoying spending time with her. In fact, idolizing her. Her laughter was infectious, and her comments were fun. She made you want to get involved in anything she approved, because you knew it would be a good time.

There he went again. It was always Cassie, Cassie, Cassie.

Stop it.

I don't have time for such emotional stuff. I had to get away. Fast.

Jake practically ran over to Charlie and Gladys and took them out for a walk around the building.

The exercise will do me good.

Watching them frolic together in the snow he said, "Well, Charlie, looks like you have a friend in Gladys forever."

The dog barked his approval, which had Jake laughing. It was like they were having a real conversation. Finally, he took them back in, secured them in their crates, and looked around. He counted twenty-five tables filled with goodies and crafts to sell, all for the farm. This was an astonishing response of the townsfolk pitching in to help a good cause. He stood in awe watching Jill and Don circulating, thanking everyone.

"Hello there." He turned to find a grey-haired, pleasant looking woman standing behind. "I'm principal Janet Lewis. I understand you're in town for a short while, but offered to help."

"Sure did. It's worth it." He reached out his hand for a shake. "I'm Jake Williams."

"It sure is worth it. And you can call me Janet."

"Thank you."

After chatting for a few minutes, he wondered if he had a new suspect for his mystery woman quest. She was about the right age and seemed genuinely nice. But as he glanced around the room at all the adults helping, he realized lots fit into that category.

He sighed.

Could be anyone. Now, get back to work.

It took five hours, but the gym was finally ready. Banners flew across the room with pictures of horses at the farm. Signs stated how people could help and advertised their wares. Slowly, people left for home, but he noticed Cassie was still talking to Jill and Don.

He had an idea.

He made a quick phone call and left in a hurry.

Sixteen

"Hey, Charlie. You can come out of your little home now." Cassie reached down and unhooked the door.

"I brought you some supper." She placed a bowl of kibble beside his water bowl.

Plopping down on a chair, still in the school gymnasium, head in hands, she let flow the tears she'd held in all day.

Drops of joy. Drops of sadness.

Her pup finished eating and put his paws on her knees, as if sensing her intense emotions.

"Here, sweetie." She pulled him up onto her lap and held on tight.

Cassie had stayed behind to make sure all the booths were finished and in good working order and that all the signs had been posted. Now all she could think about were the horses at the farm. Oh, how she loved each one of them. They were Jewel, Cutie, Edgar, Clyde, and Joy, to name a few. Each one had been rescued from a joyless existence and was now flourishing. She'd gotten to know the horses when she helped Jill muck out stalls, and particularly enjoyed brushing them, which enriched her relationships with them. She'd seen many of them arrive unkempt, restless, unhappy and emerge into confidant, glossy, healthy pets, and she loved being part of the process.

Tears continued to roll down her cheeks, but this time they were joyful for the people who had come forward to pitch in. There was a lot of kindness in this small town. She loved how everyone always came together to help one another. It was a blessing and an honor to live here, for it was like the town itself was the pot of gold at the end of the rainbow.

"I knew you'd still be here."

Startled, Cassie looked up to find Jake just inside the door. Quickly wiping her eyes, she put Charlie on the floor and jumped up.

"Just doing a few final touches," she said.

"I brought food." He moved closer. "And a latte. And Kelly added a bone for Charlie." He reached down to pat the happy pup, who was excited to see him. "I figured you'd stay to do a few things and wouldn't have time to eat."

Her stomach growled. "How kind, and you're right." She pulled another chair over. "Come and join me."

He walked over and sat. She did too.

"May I give him the bone?" he asked. "He has definitely sniffed it out."

"Go ahead." She smiled as Charlie grasped his special treat and happily ran off to a corner of the room to gnaw on it.

"Are you sure I'm not interfering?" he asked. "You seemed upset when I came in."

He must have noticed her tears.

"Oh, it's nothing. Just thinking of the horses."

"I get it. There seem to be many in need. But you've done a good job organizing a way to help them."

"Thanks. But really, everyone helped." She eyed the bags. "I hope you brought enough for two. You must be hungry, too."

"I did."

He rifled through one bag and handed her a sandwich, along with the coffee. As they sat munching, he said, “You know, Charlie’s a great pup. And I can totally understand your love for the rescued horses but I seem to recall you always being a huge animal lover and even bringing stray cats and dogs home.”

“Sure did. My dad thought I was too tender-hearted, but my parents always helped me find their families. Of course, we kept a few over the years, too.” She bit into the sandwich. “Chicken. Delicious. Thank you.”

“And I recall that sometimes the pet was sitting on their owners’ lawns, and you just imagined they were lost.” He chuckled.

She could feel a blush coming on. “You remember that?”

“Yes, I do. I also remember Mrs. Aimly seeing you walk off with her pug out having a potty break and chasing after you in her nightgown.” He shook his head. “I can still summon up how terrified you looked when you realized the dog wasn’t lost or abandoned.”

“My parents were mortified.”

“It was pretty sweet. You were just trying to help and, of course, you always gave them lots of treats. The pets thought they’d struck gold. Many of them started following you home, preferring to live with you.”

“I had a whole drawer full of dog and cat treats.” She grinned. “I had to use them up, of course.”

“Of course. By the way, is Charlie a rescue?”

“In a way. His original owner got sick and could no longer take care of him. I couldn’t resist, the moment I met him.” He wagged his tail as he looked up from the bone he was chewing, obviously hearing his name.

“I can see why.”

“I have a cat as well. Panda, also nicknamed DQ for drama queen.”

“Yeah?” He laughed.

"Yeah. She wandered into my life one day, probably sensing I was a softie and free with treats. She's a cutie but makes sure the pup knows she's the boss. Panda loves ordering Charlie around and running the show. And hey, wait a second, I also remember you assisting me in some of my rescues back then."

"I did. I even recall your dad telling you not to bring home any more pets and we smuggled a cat into our shed and kept it there for a few days, plying him with food. We took turns smuggling him into our bedrooms at night. That is, until we saw the lost posters plastered all down the street."

"Oh, I remember that well." She took a bite of her sandwich, chewing quickly. "I'm sure the cat gained ten pounds from that brief stay. He used to run out to greet us every time we walked by his house."

"Sure did. You were kind back then and you still are."

"Kind? No one beats you, donating all that money to the horse rescue." Cassie smiled. "Jill was just beside herself. You have always been very generous. I remember that about you."

She was surprised to see his face turn red. "I should have told her not to tell. But look at what you're doing." His hand gestured around the room.

"I just feel for those poor horses who are given another chance."

"Yes, second chances are important."

She got the feeling he was talking about himself. Was this a good time to ask why?

"You mentioned you hit rock bottom." She decided to just go for it. "Are you okay now?"

Silence.

Oh, no. She had pushed too hard. "I'm sorry for prying."

"You're not prying," he said slowly. "You know, I am okay now. But I wasn't for quite a while."

"I'm happy to hear that. I mean that you're okay now, not that you weren't for a while."

"Don't worry. I understood what you meant."

She stayed quiet, wondering if he would open up.

Silence, then..."Years ago my father passed away suddenly," Jake said. "A massive heart attack."

"I'm sorry to hear that." Cassie reached out and squeezed his hand.

"It was tough, since no one had a chance to say goodbye and my mother was a wreck."

Cassie remembered how close he was to his mom. As a kid, he was always helping her with stuff, carrying in groceries, shoveling the walk, even hanging up the laundry. His father worked a lot and was not home much, his brother was older and was off at school out west. Jake felt it was his duty to help. He felt he was the man of the house.

"I had moved into a condo by then," he continued. "But my mother asked if I would temporarily move back in with her to see her through the worst of it. She especially hated being alone at night." He sighed. Loudly. His eyes took on a faraway look. Cassie remained quiet, giving him the time he needed to tell his story. "One evening I was working late at night. She called me needing a carton of milk and I promised to pick it up on the way home."

He took a deep breath in and pushed it out, as he put his sandwich down.

Cassie waited him out while he rubbed his eyes, as if trying to focus. "The next I knew, the police were at my office to tell me my mother had slid off the road and hit a hydro pole. She died on the spot."

"Oh, I'm sorry." Cassie continued to hold his hand. He clasped it tighter.

"I was a lawyer at the time and dealing with a heavy-duty case that was going to trial the next day. My client had come up with new evidence that morning and I was struggling to incorporate it. I didn't think my mother's request was urgent and

I still had to put in a few more hours making sure I was ready for the next day." He paused, taking a sip of coffee.

Cassie felt herself holding her own breath and let it out slowly. This was heartbreaking.

"It was all my fault, you know. It was a snowy night and bitterly cold, and my mother went out to get the milk herself and slid on the ice. My father usually drove and even though she had a license, she hadn't driven much. She shouldn't have been out there in that weather." He shrugged. "Either she felt she needed the milk earlier or she was just bored."

It wasn't his fault, of course, but she stayed quiet. After all, blame isn't often rational and to lose his mother would have been horrendous. And just after his father as well.

"And I fell apart. I started to drink, quit my job, and ended up losing my home."

That was why he had been in that camper.

Silence.

"How did you end up in Rainbow?"

"I drove straight here where I once had good memories." He looked at her. "And it crossed my mind to try to find you."

"I wish you had. I would have been there for you."

"I know, but I was ashamed of who I'd become." He drank the last of his coffee, crumpled the cup and placed it in the garbage container beside them. "But luck was with me, and I got 'rainbowed.' My anonymous helper got me back on track. I can't tell you how much that meant to me. To be down and out and to have someone reach out to me."

"How did you end up in Manitoba?"

"Bolstered by my rainbow giver's faith in me, I called my brother on Christmas Day and he took me in. He helped me and even hooked me up with a counselor. When he offered me a job at his newspaper, I jumped at the chance, since it was my law business that had kept me from going home earlier that night. I was eager to try something else."

"So you practiced law for a while?"

"Yes. Family law. Not anymore, though."

"Do you miss it?"

"Yes. At times. I offered to look over some documents for the horse farm and admittedly felt a twinge of excitement. Jill's going to bring them to me tomorrow."

"Would you ever go back to it?"

"Maybe."

She leaned over and gave him a hug. "It really wasn't your fault, you know."

"Thanks." He hugged her back. "I know that now. Counseling helped a lot. I would have brought that milk home and my mother knew that. She was probably restless and wanting to do something. But upon reflection, I realized I was too engrossed in my work."

"Sounds like it was important, though."

"But family is always first. I see how my brother makes a point of always being with his wife and kids for dinner and getting home at a reasonable hour. Not me. I would stay up nights working on my law cases and now I'm always running around chasing stories."

"I see that. I mean, you came all the way to Rainbow to chase one."

He laughed. "I did. And besides, I don't have a family to come home to since I live alone. But I do know work can't be everything."

"Finding balance is hard. I often struggle with that."

"It sure is. I do enjoy reporting, though. The thrill of the hunt, such as trying to track down my mystery helper."

"I saw you checking everyone out tonight as if they were a possible suspect."

"You caught me, and also, you know me well. I was wondering if it was the principal. She's around the right age."

He looked at her as if expecting her to say something about that. Agree or disagree.

"You should just leave it alone, you know." She knew she sounded angry, but couldn't help it. She also pulled her hand away. "As I've said before, he or she obviously wants to remain anonymous. You should respect that."

"Kelly said the same thing. You're totally against me seeking out the woman who helped me?"

"Yes. You could write about how kind this town is, not just single out one person. Especially since they want to be anonymous. You're trying to reveal something no one wants revealed. It isn't fair or right."

She stood, hands curled into fists, and glared at him.

Seventeen

Uh-oh.

Cassie was sure to walk out the door soon. It seemed to be in the town script.

Jake was surprised. His eyes dropped.

She sounded and looked angry. Really angry.

She must know who did it and was protecting her. Why else would she react so strongly?

Of course, once again, maybe she represented the thoughts of the whole town—they wanted it kept secret. Left alone. Maybe they all knew. After all, Holly sounded angry, too. Not to mention Kelly.

His head swirled with the one constant question he couldn't find an answer to.

Why was it kept quiet?

What was the big deal?

He didn't understand it.

This mystery woman had literally saved his life and now he found she helped others as well. Surely this woman should be applauded for all the good work she does. He longed to hear her story and why she rainbowed people. She deserved recognition and just maybe people would emulate her more and pass on her good intentions. This would definitely make the world a better place.

Why was it all so secretive?

Or...once again, the thought hit him that maybe no one really knew, just suspected, and respected this person's decision to do things in silence.

This was the hardest story he'd ever worked on. Usually by now someone would have leaked something. Not this time.

Also, normally, if people seemed resistant to his questions and it was not a big deal, he would just forget about the story and leave it alone. Drop it completely. But he had promised his brother a really good Christmas article and he couldn't let him down.

"I'd really like to thank her," he stated emphatically, finally finding the words to say. He'd expected her to leave, like all the rest, but she still stood, staring him down. "I'd love to throw her a big party to celebrate who she is and the good work she does."

"But you're not listening." She stamped her foot. "As I said before, maybe she doesn't want to be thanked.

"But maybe she does. Maybe she's waiting for someone to find her. To out her. Please." He patted the seat beside him. "Why don't you sit with me, and we can talk this out."

He figured this would be when she'd walk out, but she surprised him by sitting.

"You know," he said. "I thought it was you for a while until I realized the person has been doing it for a long time. She'd have to be older than us."

"It makes no difference. You have no right to come to Rainbow and cause a disturbance."

A disturbance?

Staring into Cassie's eyes and seeing unmistakable pain there, and a hint of more tears, he realized she was right.

I have no right to intrude. Besides, I'm enjoying our reconnection and feel much better having told her about my past. I can't blow this second chance. I really miss our friendship.

He couldn't do it.

No, he wouldn't do it.

If, for some reason writing this story would hurt her, as well as others, he needed to just let it go.

There had to be an explanation as to why no one wanted the woman's identity out. Either they didn't know or simply didn't want him to know. But it looked like he'd never find out. Odd, since it was a lovely story about a rainbow giver and being rainbowed.

"Okay, I won't," he said. Surely, his brother would understand. He'd come up with another story.

"Promise?"

"Promise."

"Pinky-swear?"

"Pinky-swear." They entangled their baby fingers just like they had as kids.

"Sorry. I shouldn't have been that harsh, especially when you were confiding in me about your mother," she said.

"No problem. It was obviously on your mind, and I appreciate honesty."

"Well, speaking of pinky-swearing and honesty," Cassie said. "I'm going to be even more straightforward."

"Please, go ahead."

"Here goes. I'm still upset that you left without saying goodbye all those years ago. I was heartbroken."

What?

"I don't understand what you mean." Was she joking? Trying to change the topic?

"You moved and never told me. We were best buds and back then we pinky-swore as well that we'd always tell the truth and always be friends."

"Yes, and I stood by that." Why was she looking at him with eyes that accused and judged him at the same time? And was that a tear popping out?

"Oh, c'mon. You left me in the lurch wondering what happened to you."

"I did not." Surely, she was just teasing. "I did say goodbye. Okay, it wasn't in person because we took off fast, but I left you my address. If anyone should be hurt, it would be me. And I was. I was disappointed you never wrote me."

Her eyes were wide as she grimaced. "But you didn't give me your address."

"Wait a second." He leaned back in his chair, trying to grasp what she was saying. Then it dawned on him. "You didn't check our tree? I actually took a huge risk and sneaked out in the middle of the night and left you a message in the tree. My dad would have grounded me for months if he had found out. But I did it anyway."

"What?"

"I left you a note in our tree. You remember our special tree, don't you?"

"Well, yes, of course." He watched as understanding hit her. "Oh, no. I never went near that tree again. It was our special place and it hurt too much."

"I thought you'd check it. I never imagined you wouldn't. And I didn't write you first, figuring you had given up on us. I didn't want to push my friendship on you." He took hold of her hand and surprisingly she didn't resist. "You know, I bet it's still there. It rained that night and I wrapped it in plastic. C'mon, let's go check."

"I doubt it'd be there now. A lot of years have passed."

"Let's look, anyway. If only to prove I did what I said."

"Okay. You've piqued my curiosity. I guess it won't hurt. C'mon, Charlie."

They locked up and walked to the forest behind their childhood homes. Once again, it was nearby, so Cassie left her car in the school parking lot.

"Look, it's snowing again," Cassie said. "Seems to do that every time you're around."

"It looks that way." Jake laughed, glancing around, drinking it all in. He hadn't seen these woods since he was a kid and was delighted to see the white crystals descend on the branches, making the trees sparkle, appearing magical. "It's like the forest is dressing up for us in special evening clothes."

"You're right. It all looks incredibly beautiful." She laughed. "And look at Charlie. He just loves the snow."

"He sure does." The pup was busy trying to catch snowflakes in his mouth, biting at them, stopping every few minutes to roll in it. "But I didn't expect all this extra growth. There are definitely a few more trees since I was here last. I'm not sure where ours is."

"I remember exactly where it is."

Cassie led him right to it. Their special tree had a large hidey-hole that was hidden by branches. They used to leave each other messages regularly, pretending they were spies on secret missions.

"That's it. I remember it now. Go ahead, check it, Cassie."

She reached in, felt around. "Looks like a few nests have inhabited the tree. Oh, I think I feel some plastic." She dragged out a small package. Shaking the leaves and twigs off it, she could see it was clearly an envelope wrapped in plastic. Her name was written there, and she recognized the writing. It was Jake's.

"No way," she said. "I can't believe I never thought to come here. I'm sorry I judged you harshly."

Jake smiled. "And I'm sorry I didn't write you anyway and we could have sorted this out years ago. But at least you know I tried to reach you. Go on, open it."

"Nah. I think I'll take it home, if you don't mind. The way the snow is coming down, it'll get really wet and ruined in seconds."

"You're right. The snow definitely is picking up."

He walked her back to her car.

"Are you sure you don't want a ride?"

"No, the fresh air is doing me good. I hope you get some sleep tonight," he said. "You're probably nervous about tomorrow."

"You remember how I can't sleep the night before events or tests?"

"I do."

He stared at her looking all pretty, hair tousled, baseball cap askew, big, fat snowflakes framing her face.

I want to kiss her.

To hold her close and never let her go.

Cassie represents all that had been good in my life.

Don't do it.

She gave no indication she wanted more, and kissing her would probably send her running.

I can't chance it.

"Well, see you tomorrow," she said, turning to open her car door.

Good. The moment was gone.

"I'll be there." He patted Charlie on his head, waited until they drove off, then headed home.

On the walk back, he felt relieved he'd told her what happened to him. Her support was sincere and just made him feel better. A memory flashed, and he remembered one of the last times he had seen her.

Cassie used to carry a bright pink knapsack everywhere. There always seemed to be snacks in it, especially cookies. One day after school, he had heard her screaming out in the playground, "Leave me alone. Leave me alone." He had raced over and saw Stuart White, one of the school's biggest bullies, grab her knapsack and take off with it, yelling, "Thanks for the grub."

Sobbing, Cassie had collapsed on the grass, hands over her face. Without a moment's thought that Stuart was in the eighth grade and twice his size, Jake ran after him, tackled him in a nearby park, and managed to get her precious knapsack back intact. He later thought the only reason Stuart backed off was that they both took karate, and the bully knew Jake was more advanced. In other words, he knew Jake could overtake him in seconds.

But when he ran back to where Cassie had been, she was gone.

Taking it to her porch, he leaned it against her door and rang the bell. Then he ran. He was too shy to give it to her by himself, not wanting the attention or any fuss being made over him, but he watched from a distance as Cassie opened the door, looked around, then noticed the knapsack. The most beautiful smile ever appeared on her face as she picked it up and stood there hugging it. It made his day. But when he got home, his parents informed him they were moving fast, effective early the next day. He'd never seen that smile again.

Until now.

It was worth waiting for.

Arriving back at the bed and breakfast, he let himself in and hurried to his room. He checked his emails. There was one from his brother. *"Call me even if it's late."*

He called.

"I need that story, Jake. Membership is down again. I need something different."

Jake rolled his eyes. "I can't do it."

"But you promised."

"I did. But things have changed."

Silence.

"Please, I need it."

Jake had never heard his brother sound so sad or desperate. Or beg. He was caught in the middle, but he now knew what he had to do. "Okay, I'll keep trying." He just couldn't let him down.

Guilt surfaced.

Yes, he had to write that story. Yes, the rainbow giver had saved his life, but his brother had never let him down and had helped him get back on his own two feet. He had been a major part of his survival and had even gone to Alcohol Anonymous meetings with him. He'd just have to tell Cassie he couldn't honor their pinky-swear. Once he explained, he was sure she'd understand and hopefully see it the way he did—that everyone deserved to be thanked.

Didn't they?

Now...to amp up his search.

Hey, mystery woman, you won't evade me for much longer. Count on it.

Eighteen

I'll never forget the day I received a package from Mom.

After she had passed.

It was pretty freaky. Unimaginable.

My dad brought it home from the lawyer's office.

He'd had no idea Mom had left this for me.

I didn't want to open it at first, fearing the contents, but knowing my mother would never hurt me, I decided to see what was in it. I can still recall my hands shaking as I slowly ripped off the brown wrapping paper and lifted the lid.

The first thing I saw was a raggedy, worn, multi-colored teddy bear. He was missing an eye but looked well-loved. He sat on top of a letter from my mother, and a large photograph of my grandmother, who had passed away before I was born. I had seen enough photos of her to recognize her. There was also a framed story signed by my granny, written in beautiful calligraphy.

I carried the letter everywhere I went. The photo of my grandmother and the story hung in my home office, and the teddy resided on my desk. On the door was my mother's sign, simply stating that this was 'My Sacred Place. Just like my mom's, no one ever entered except me. I later hung a picture of my mother as well, happy to have both women smiling down at me, inspiring me every time I gazed at them.

Feeling nostalgic, I reached into my pocket for my wallet, opened it up, and pulled out the letter.

My dog scooted closer and licked my face. He seemed to know that these moments sitting on a bench by the river were rooted in memories of my mom. And he wanted me to understand he was there for me. Always.

I unfolded the letter. It was rumpled and smudged with tearstains, but I read it often. Tonight was one of those nights when I needed to feel closer to her. Especially since someone visiting the town still seemed eager to expose me.

To my dear little girl,

Hello, sweetheart.

If you have received this letter, it means I'm not here. I instructed my lawyer to give this to you when I've passed. I wanted you to hear the truth of what I've been doing directly from me.

But shhhhh...it's a secret. No one must know.

As you know, my father—your grandpa—passed away when I was six years old. Although we lived in a tiny apartment and made do with very little, I never wanted for anything and felt completely loved.

That Christmas, I spotted a multicolored rainbow teddy bear sitting in the window of a local store window. He had a tuft of bright pink hair and I fell in love with him, because he reminded me of my dad—bright and cheery and always happy. I even called him Poppy after him because that was what I called my dad.

I just knew he belonged to me.

I used to stand in front of that window and stare at Poppy, and say to my mom over and over, "Santa will bring me this. I can't wait." I was sure Poppy would be coming home to live with me.

I didn't know at the time that my mother had no money to buy me any gift, let alone an expensive, gorgeous teddy bear.

But sure enough, he did.

Poppy came to live with me on Christmas Day.

I was excited at unwrapping him, thinking Santa was the best ever.

Years later, I found out from my mom that she didn't have the money to buy him for me. She figured someone had obviously overheard me and left the teddy bear outside our apartment door on Christmas Eve.

Anonymously.

Apparently, they rang the doorbell and when my mom answered, there was no one there but a package.

Mom never found out who did this, and she told me how she cried and cried, knowing she could give me the best gift ever. One I wanted badly. She never forgot that special night when the kindness of a stranger changed her whole life.

Later, when things fared better, she wanted to give back.

To do to others what had been done to her. To be a light in their darkness.

Your grandmother was really creative, and she created a rainbow basket campaign for herself, where she left little gifts in multi-colored baskets for people in need of support.

All anonymously.

Just like the bear had been left anonymously that special Christmas.

People in the community began to call the gift giving' rainbowing' people and the ones who received the gifts were termed 'rainbowed.'

But just like Gramma never found out who left the teddy bear, no one knew she was doing the giving.

It was all a secret. A secret of love. When you read her story, you will understand more.

Oh, another interesting thing, Gramma just didn't do this at Christmas. As a matter of fact, she always left one Christmas ornament up all year round. As you recall, I did the same. I know you often wondered why a nutcracker, or the creche, or an angel ornament often stayed put, long after we put the decorations away. I'd always say, "One day I'll tell you." Then I think you just forgot about it because you were used to it. Well, today is that one day. It's time for you to know. Here's the reason. It is to remind us that the kindness felt and given at Christmas should not just be centered on one day but should extend all year round. She rainbowed people, no matter what the season.

Oh, and when my mother passed, she had sent me a letter to read after, just like I am doing for you.

She also had written in calligraphy and framed her reasons behind all her giving. I left you her story so you could read it from her own heart. That way, you will understand even more.

I continued her legacy.

And so, my dear daughter, I am hoping you will as well.

Giving from the heart, when no one else knows, brought me great peace in life.

Also, please know, gifts don't have to be big things or expensive. A chocolate bar, a movie, a book. It's really the thought that counts.

This is the way I have lived, just like my mom, choosing to get up each morning and try to love in the minutes of my life, largely unseen, and unknown.

But hey, I also don't want you to feel pressure if life calls you in another direction. Follow your heart, always.

My darling girl. Please know that I may not be with you physically, but I am always in your heart.

Know that I love you, am proud of you always, and please, let your light shine. Never hide it or bury it. And always remember, I will love you forever.

All my love, Mom

I folded the letter and slid it back inside my wallet.

Tears rolled, recalling how I had then read my grandmother's words, which helped me understand even more.

I loved their philosophy—to love and give in the minutes of our lives.

And I know my mother and grandmother would especially be proud that I had decided at Mom's funeral to continue what turned out was their work before I even received the letter.

We were all united in love. All of one heart.

We also both had added our own touches.

My grandmother used multi-colored baskets, and I discovered my mother included the rainbow cards, while I created a bracelet. Both of us added the words 'you are loved' to our contributions.

I loved helping in the silence of the night when times could be dark and no one expected anything.

It needed to remain silent.

No reporting in the news.

Ever.

I would see to that.

Nineteen

"Well, Charlie, today is the day. Joyfest," Cassie said, sitting on the edge of the bed. "Let's hope we raise lots of money for all our horse friends now, and for the many more to come."

Her pup woofed and wagged his tail, making her smile. Panda just stretched and eyed her as if saying, "Must you interrupt me? I'm trying to sleep."

In truth, Cassie was exhausted.

She had opened the envelope Jake had left her all those years ago and couldn't get over what was there. Then, she couldn't sleep.

First there was the letter. Short and to the point.

Hey Cassie,

Just found out Dad got a new job, and we have to leave early tomorrow morning. I wanted to run over to your house and say goodbye, but Mom said we have no time and that I have to pack. But I sneaked out the window in the middle of the night and ran to our favorite tree. I know you'll check there when you find out I'm gone. We have to keep in touch. You're my best friend in the whole wide world.

Jake

He had added his new address and shockingly taped to the letter a chain he wore around his neck all the time. He had explained to her once that his grandpa had given it to him, and she knew it held a lot of sentimental value. The fact he wanted her to have it touched her enormously, and to think it had been in that tree all those years.

She sighed. Loudly.

Thank goodness it had been kept safe. Jake had been smart to cover it all with plastic. She sure wished she had checked that tree back then. She should have known he wouldn't have left without saying goodbye.

It also would have been wonderful to have kept in touch and just maybe he would have phoned her when things had turned bad for him. She didn't even know his father had died and later his mother, and she was broken-hearted that he had felt all alone during that time, blaming himself. Maybe she could have listened to him and hugged him and guided him, so he didn't drink and lose his job and his home. She probably was crediting herself with way too much influence—after all, they might have lost touch anyway as the years sped by—but she sure wished she'd known all of this. It was just horrific that he had gone through all of that alone.

Charlie nudged her leg.

"Yes, I know, sweetie. You've been out for a potty break, eaten breakfast, and it's time to get ready to go to the school." She patted his head. "And here I am, just sitting here reminiscing."

He was like her little alarm clock, knowing when she had to be up and about.

Glancing at her watch, she got up and dressed quickly.

"C'mon, Charlie. Let's get going. Looks like I'll have to forgo my usual stop at the café. Oh, well, I can grab a coffee at the fundraiser." She snapped on his leash. "And Panda, remember, you're in charge of the apartment when I'm gone." Panda never even opened her eyes. She made Cassie smile. A burglar could storm in, escape with the goods, and as long as Panda had food and water, she'd sleep through it. Such was the life of a cat or, at least, her cat. But she loved Panda no matter what. Her purring alone always managed to calm Cassie and reminded her to slow down and enjoy the day.

Better get going.

She had gotten permission to bring Charlie, so she loaded his crate in the car, grabbed more food for him, along with his water dish, and they set off. Of course, it only took minutes to get to the school, and after pulling in, she quickly jumped out and opened the back door.

"Here you go. Now let's get your crate."

She led Charlie to the front door, opened it, and hit the buttons to shut off the alarm. She then turned the lights on as she went down the hallway to the gymnasium, aware the volunteers and vendors would be arriving soon.

"Good morning. How are you doing?"

Startled, she turned to see Jake holding out a coffee cup. He must have come in shortly after she did. "One latte for you. Kelly said you hadn't been in yet."

Just the smell of vanilla mixed with caffeine made her salivate.

Putting the crate down, she took the cup, set it down, and threw her arms around him.

"You are a lifesaver," she said.

Pulling back, she realized his mouth was opened in shock.

"I'll bring you more coffee if I get this response every time. You surprise me."

She could feel her face burning. "I'll do anything for a latte. But not only do I thank you for the coffee, but for saying goodbye to me all those years ago." She pulled the chain out of her pocket. "And you gave me this. But I must give it back. It was your grandfather's."

"No, no. I want you to have it. That's how much I valued our friendship."

"But I really let you down." She felt guilty. "And we lost many years."

"We did, but we can stay in touch now. That is, if you'd like that."

"I would. Definitely."

She almost swooned at his big, charming grin and felt like hugging him again.

Stop it.

Remember. Manitoba was quite a distance.

"Well, I'll put the chain on. That way I won't lose it," she said quickly.

"Let me help." And he reached behind her neck to fasten it.

And yes, his touch gave her goosebumps. Even a few shivers, just like romance books declare could happen. Sometimes they actually get it right. But enough of this, they needed to get to work.

Ignore those feelings.

"Well, everyone will be here soon. I'd better get moving," she said, turning away.

"So..." He looked around. "Any last-minute tasks for me?"

"Well, I'm just wandering around making sure we're ready." She could hear car doors slamming shut. "I think that's the volunteers arriving. The vendors, too."

"Well remember, I'm here for you. Let me know what I can do."

"Thank you. I will."

She quickly settled Charlie in his crate. "You can see everything here," she crooned, "And don't worry, I'll be by to let you out."

"Just like last time, I can take him out as well, if you'd like," Jake said, strolling over. "Jill said she was bringing Gladys, too, and I promised to take care of her."

"That'd be great." Charlie barked his approval. "Oh, there's Gladys now and she's running right to you."

"Hi, you two," Jill yelled out.

"Hi there," Cassie and Jake spoke at the same time. She laughed when Gladys broke free from Jill's hand and jumped up on Jake, who swooped her up in his arms. That seemed to be their thing. Gladys ran to Jake, he pulled her into his arms where she covered his face with kisses, then gazed at him with such love. It was really sweet to watch.

"Definitely a love affair going on there," Jill whispered to Cassie.

"You're right about that."

"I just can't thank you enough for doing all this," Jill said, hugging Cassie tightly. "Don will be here in a moment. He had a few chores to take care of." Her voice lowered. "And a costume to put on."

Cassie laughed. "No problem."

"Sorry, I had to bring Gladys. She can't stand being alone. Hope that's okay. The principal said it was."

"Sure it is. I have the same problem. You know, I brought an exercise pen, just in case," Cassie said. "Would that work? That way, they can play together instead of being in separate crates. It's out in my trunk."

Jill nodded. "That's a good idea. The more socializing Gladys undergoes, the better."

"Sorry, but I can't help but overhear you," Jake said. "I can run out and get it, if you'd like."

Cassie gave him her keys and, after handing Gladys over to Jill, he took off and was back in minutes.

They all helped set it up and after she added water and a few chew toys, they placed the two dogs in it. Immediately, Charlie and Gladys started running around in their little area, looking happy to be together.

"They seem like they're already best buddies," Cassie said. "I'm glad they met the other day. They'll have a great time."

"I can guarantee that," Jill said, looking around. "I see most of the vendors are here already."

"Yes," Cassie said. "I love all the excitement just before an event begins. The smell of coffee percolating, popcorn popping, people chatting."

"Me, too." Jill nodded. "I'm touched by everyone pitching in to help. I'm going to go around and thank all the people in the booths again. I'm absolutely astounded at the amazing turn-out."

"I'll join you," Cassie said. Jill looked ready to cry and probably needed a lot of support. She totally understood. The love this town had for her work with horses really was incredible.

"And how about I stick around with the pups for a bit to make sure they continue to get along and settle down?" Jake asked.

"Good idea," Cassie said. "Thanks." Jake was still the thoughtful guy she remembered.

"Oh," Jill said. "Jake, here are those papers you said you'd look over." She pulled a brown envelope out of her tote and handed them to him.

"I'll get right on that tonight," he promised.

"I appreciate it."

Cassie noticed his face lit up and she remembered he had offered to check out some legal papers for Jill. Seemed like he was eager to work on them. Maybe he missed being a lawyer more than he thought, considering he had studied all those years to be called to the bar.

"Well, let's get going," Jill said, pulling her out of her thoughts.

Cassie and Jill started making the rounds. She was searching for Lainey and found her setting up a beanbag toss game.

"How are you doing?" Cassie asked. "Big day today."

Lainey's beaming face said it all. "Oh, it's so exciting, miss." Her black pigtails flew back and forth as she gazed around the room. "To see a dream actually come true is the best thing ever."

"It sure is," Cassie said. "And remember, this is all your doing."

"Oh, not all. Everyone helped."

"Yes," Jill piped in. "But you dreamed first. Thank you with all my heart. Group hug, please."

They all joined, just as the doors opened and people poured in.

"Showtime," Lainey whispered. "I'm excited but scared."

"It'll go well," Cassie said. "Just you watch and make sure you take the time to enjoy it all."

"There's Don," Jill said.

Cassie looked over to see Santa Claus walking through the gymnasium, a big smile on his face, and many 'Ho, ho, ho's' ringing out. She'd almost forgotten Don was Santa today, which was perfect, considering he looked just like him.

Jill ran over to greet him and led him to an area they had roped off where children could sit on his knee, tell him their wishes, and have their pictures taken. Cassie noted there was already a line-up there, while she continued walking around, making sure everything ran smoothly. She smiled at the crowds of people buying last minute Christmas gifts and enjoyed watching her students taking care of little ones with games and races and even face painting. There were a lot of little elves and reindeer running around. They had come up with the idea that they would offer free babysitting for parents while they shopped. Judging by the large number of children, it was a huge success. She also found herself glancing over at Jake from time to time, noticing how easy he was with people. Considering he was only in town a short while, it was pretty great of him to help out.

"It's going well," Jake said, coming over as if aware of her perusal. "I just took Charlie and Gladys out and they're both snoozing away."

"Thanks. That's one good thing about pups. They sleep a lot."

"Sure do. But when they're awake, they're wild things. I didn't think I was going to get them to come back in. They were having fun rolling around in the snow."

"Aha. Did Charlie con you into throwing the ball over and over?"

"Sure did. Over and over and over." He rubbed his arm. "Ouch, the pain."

Cassie laughed. "Yep, that's Charlie's favorite thing. He'll wear you right out."

"Gladys too, apparently." He pointed to Kelly's booth. "Would you like to join me for some pie? I've been hearing people walk by me exclaiming about how good the apple pie is."

"I'd love to."

They sat at a table facing the room. "One latte coming up and one plain coffee, right?" Kelly asked, walking over.

Cassie nodded. "You got it and two pieces of pie."

"This is really nice," Jake said, looking around.

"Yes, the Rainbow community is astounding. They always come together to help each other."

"I can see why you wouldn't want to leave."

"Me, neither," Kelly said, carrying a tray with the coffees and pieces of pie. "I couldn't help overhearing you. I could never leave this place."

"I'm going to have a hard time saying goodbye," Jake said.

"Would you ever consider staying?" Kelly asked.

"I sure have thought about it." Jake nodded, taking a bite of the pie. "This is delicious, by the way."

"Thanks," Kelly said.

Cassie searched his face, wondering if he'd say more. Would he actually move back? She couldn't believe how happy she felt to hear that.

Suddenly, there was a shout of joy and Lainey came running over. "We've got a final total for donations, Ms. Blackburn, and it's incredible news."

Cassie glanced at her watch. "Well, the fundraiser is over shortly. How about we announce it to the whole room? It'll make everyone happy."

"Good idea," Jake said. "Maybe it will inspire even more donations."

"Well," Kelly pointed to their plates. "Hate to sound like a mom here but finish your pie first."

Excited, Cassie gulped her coffee down, scarfed down the pie, and went with Lainey to the stage area.

"May I have everyone's attention," Cassie said into the microphone. "I'm asking Jill to please join us on stage and everyone else to gather around." Don was still Santa and still busy so he obviously couldn't come. She then handed the microphone to Lainey.

"No, you do it," Lainey said, her voice shaky.

"I think you should be the one," Cassie said. "You're the main organizer."

"What are we up here for?" Jill asked.

"To announce how much money we raised," Lainey said.

"Oh." Jill squeezed Lainey's hand. "You can do it. I'd like that."

Lainey began quietly, then got stronger. "Thanks everyone for helping out and making dreams come true for these special horses. I am pleased to announce that we have raised fifty thousand dollars and we're still going strong."

Everyone cheered and Jill burst into tears. Cassie wrapped one arm around her and draped her other one over Lainey's shoulder.

"Good job," she said, just as Jill reached out and pulled the two of them into another group hug. "Thank you."

Don't cry. Don't cry. Don't cry.

I have to oversee the cleanup.

I couldn't help it.

Clyde and Cutie and Jewel and all the horses Jill had saved tiptoed across my heart. They would continue to live rich, full lives and new ones would join them. They would be saved.

Okay, cry. After all, they were tears of love.

Cassie couldn't believe how fast the cleanup went. With everyone pitching in, they had everything sparkling and put away in a little over an hour.

She watched as Jake said goodbye to Gladys and she got Charlie ready to go home.

Looking up, she saw Jake watching her.

"I felt proud to be a part of this," he said.

"Me, too. Did you drive over?"

"No. Walked."

"Would you like a lift home? The snow is really coming down."

"Sure. After all, I seem to be the one making it snow all the time. It's a gift."

Cassie laughed. "I know."

He helped her carry the last few things to the car and then she took off, nice and slow. The roads still needed to be plowed.

"Remember how we used to make snow angels?" Jake asked, chuckling.

"Sure do." She pulled into the bed and breakfast. "Mom would get mad that I'd arrive home with wet clothes."

"Yeah, mine too, but we sure had fun."

"Yes, we did." She came to a stop.

"Well thank you for the lift," he said, patting Charlie on the head, then getting out.

"Thank you for all your help." She started to pull away, stopped, and jumped out. "Wait a second." Releasing Charlie, she raced by Jake and jumped into a huge snow patch.

"I'm never too old to make a snow angel."

"Best idea ever." He plopped down beside her, with Charlie running back and forth between them.

After they finished, he helped her up.

It feels good holding Jake's hand and just having pure lighthearted fun.

Just like old times.

I don't want it to end.

"Oh, I forgot to ask. What are you doing on Christmas Day?" she asked.

"Not much."

"Would you like to join us? My parents will be back tomorrow morning."

"Sure. I'd like that."

To her surprise, he leaned down and kissed her cheek.

"See you tomorrow," he said, helping her put Charlie back in the car.

Waving goodbye, she touched her cheek. It was burning.

Oh, it felt good to be around him again.

Darn.

There were those goosebumps again.

Twenty

Jake couldn't sleep.

It was Christmas Eve and he sat by the window sipping the hot chocolate Holly had thoughtfully left in a thermos in his room. Staring out, he watched the wind toss swirls of snowflakes along the river path. At times all he saw was a white blizzard, which was actually quite beautiful, as long as you weren't out in it. Gold and silver Christmas lights shone through all the whiteness and if he were an artist, he would paint what he saw, and title it 'hope.'

Thinking of hope, it'd been a terrific day.

The fundraiser was a huge success, the horse farm would thrive under the numerous cash donations, and he got to spend the day with Cassie. Once again, it was like they were ten, where they used to spend all their time together and accomplished many things as a team. Like picking up groceries for Mrs. Stephens when she broke her leg, or shoveling the driveway for Mr. Wray, who was getting up there in years.

One thing was running true, though.

He no longer felt like a kid when he looked into Cassie's eyes. It had been all he could do not to kiss her at the gym, and when she drove him home, he literally had to stop himself from leaning over and embracing her when they were playing in the snow.

Not a good idea.

Then there was the other thing that had happened tonight.

As promised, he looked over Jill and Don's legal papers for the farm. He was surprised he had offered, since he had pushed his law career away. Figuratively hid it in a part of his brain covered in cobwebs, never to be looked at again. He had wanted to forget about it, especially that he had been heavily involved in a case the night his mother passed away. Journalism saved him. The active role it played, getting him out and about in the community on the search for stories, healed him.

But looking through those papers tonight stirred up his love of all things law and the challenges it represented.

He finally had to admit he missed it. He missed helping people through legal situations and guiding them with mounds of paperwork.

He also missed this small town.

Rainbow was a special place, and he had all sorts of wonderful memories of living there. And he saw how incredible it was tonight when the whole town came out to help one of their own. You were never alone here. Townsfolks saw to that.

He was glad he'd come and especially happy he'd renewed his friendship, or to be more truthful, his crush on Cassie. He just wished he hadn't lost touch all those years.

Christmas Eve.

He sipped the last of the chocolate and started in on a gingerbread cookie, recalling that Christmas Eve five years ago when he had been depressed. Hard to believe that tonight he was downing cookies and chocolate, when on that fateful night he was swigging from bottles of whiskey.

Then along came the rainbow giver to save him.

Wait a second.

He leaned closer to the window, trying to peer through the snow.

Was someone walking along the river?

With a dog running beside him/her?

The person was bundled up and the coat's furry hood blocked their face, but the dog...A blast of wind cleared the air for a second. He knew that dog.

It was Charlie.

Which meant the bundled-up, hooded woman was Cassie.

But it couldn't be.

He had just said good night to her not that long ago.

What was she doing out again?

He rubbed his eyes. He must be imagining it. Summoning her up out of wishful thinking. She wouldn't be out walking in a blizzard.

Would she?

He opened his eyes just as he saw the person slip, try to right herself and...oh, no.

Down she went. Tumbling in the snow. This time not to make snow angels.

Charlie barked his alarm and began running frantically around her in circles.

Throwing on his coat and boots, Jake grabbed the toboggan sitting out on the porch and raced over to help. It took longer than he thought due to the wind and snow, which blinded him at times.

"Are you okay?" he asked, leaning down, brushing the snow from her face, the other hand petting Charlie, trying to reassure him.

"I don't know." She looked up, blinking fast. "Oh, it's Jake. I think I twisted my ankle."

He ran his hands over it, although it was hard to tell anything with her boots on.

"C'mon. I've brought the toboggan. Let's get you out of this storm and over to the bed and breakfast where I can really take a look at your ankle."

"You brought a sleigh?" She grinned. "Now that's quick thinking. But I think I can walk. Or at least limp."

"Better not chance it." He moved the toboggan closer and helped her slide onto it. To his surprise, Charlie jumped on, too.

"Charlie, get off," Cassie said. "It'll make it heavier for Jake to pull."

"No problem." Jake picked up the bag she was carrying and placed it on her lap. "He's just trying to protect you and doesn't want to leave your side."

After making sure she was on with no chance of falling off, he said, "Well, here goes."

Slowly, they made it across the road and to the bed and breakfast.

"Now, the stairs." Leaning on him, she could hop up, taking one step at a time, until Jake, noticing the pain in her eyes, swept her up in his arms and carried her safely to his room and eased her down on a chair, a worried Charlie following closely the whole time.

"Thanks," Cassie whispered.

"Let's get those boots off." He pulled them slowly off and rolled up the pants on her left leg.

"I think you need to see a doctor," he said. "It's already swelling and turning black and blue."

"I'm okay. I can still wiggle it back and forth."

"You might need an x-ray."

"If it still hurts tomorrow, I'll go. I promise."

Not wanting to argue, he said, "Well, Holly showed me the kitchen here and said to help myself anytime. I'll go see if there is an ice pack to take down some of that swelling."

"Just for a bit, though. I have things to do."

Things to do? In a blizzard? On Christmas Eve?

He shook his head as he took off fast and luckily found an ice pack hiding behind a roast in the freezer. Grabbing a clean towel out of the closet, he got back to the room in record time and wrapped it around her ankle.

"Remember. I've got to get going soon, Jake."

"Just wait a little more. Let the ice pack do its thing."

"But while you were gone, I tested it out and I can walk. I think I just twisted it and I'm okay now."

"Please, humor me, and give the ice a try."

She settled back in her chair. "Okay, just for a while."

He picked her bag off the nearby chair and sat beside her. As he put it down, he noticed a pink basket handle peeking out.

His heart pounded.

What?

Twenty-one

Jake had heard that saying 'time stood still,' but he had never experienced it until then.

It was as if everything around him quieted and he was locked in a moment as memories hit hard.

Closing his eyes, he recalled the first time he had seen his own pink basket hanging off his truck's mirror.

It was a miracle in his life.

It was also just like this one.

His eyes popped open.

He couldn't help himself.

It was as if something had taken hold of him, and he leaned down and opened the bag further. There were actually three baskets, and in each one held several gifts wrapped in Christmas paper, plus a warming bag.

He knew what was inside.

A Christmas dinner.

No way.

He sucked in his breath, then let it out slowly.

It couldn't just be a coincidence.

He looked over at Cassie, sitting quietly petting Charlie.

Was she the rainbow giver? The one who had saved his life?

He shook his head.

No, she couldn't be.

She was way too young.

Maybe not.

He had to know.

Pushing his chair closer, he took hold of her hand. "It *was* you," he said softly.

"Pardon?" She looked up, her face clearly puzzled.

"You rainbowed me. You are the one who helped me back then."

Her eyes dropped. "No, I..." her voice trailed off.

"Please don't deny it. I can see the baskets here with the gifts and food. Just like the one I had."

Silence then, "Yes. It was me." She looked up and stared him in the eyes.

More silence.

He couldn't quite grasp the fact it had been Cassie all along.

"You saved my life," he finally said.

"No, I didn't, Jake." She squeezed his hand. "You did."

"But it was you who made me feel worthwhile again. Did you know it was me in that truck?"

"Of course, I didn't. If I had, I would have knocked, wanting to talk to you. To help you in person. To help you more."

"But you did." He paused. "You helped me a lot. And many other people, too. But how could you have done it years ago? Before you were even born? Is there a team of people here who do this kind of thing on a regular basis?"

He watched Cassie cuddle her pup as she stared out the window. She stayed quiet and he did as well, sensing she was struggling about whether to explain the whole rainbowing process to him.

He waited her out.

Finally she spoke, telling him all about her mother and grandmother's rainbow legacy. She even pulled out the letter she carried in her wallet and let him read it, explaining her grandmother's story was framed and hanging in her office.

"You have quite the mother and grandmother," he said. "What true inspirations." To his surprise, a tear dripped down his cheek at the love that had filtered down through Cassie's family.

"They sure are."

"They made a difference in many lives, and to think, you've continued their work."

"Yes, I've tried to."

He shook his head, struggling to clear out the confusion. "But I thought your parents were away. I didn't realize your mother had passed."

"Yes, and my dad remarried. I call her Mom, too."

"Oh. I'm sorry to hear you lost your mother. I know you were really close to her." He squeezed her hand.

"It was tough, definitely."

"But what dog did you have? Charlie is a pup." He still couldn't comprehend it had been Cassie all those years ago.

"It was my other dog, Rico. He passed away."

"Oh. Sorry to hear that, too." He paused, thinking things through. "Do most people around here know that you do this?"

"I don't think so. Especially since it's been going on for such a long time. Like you, they suspect someone older."

"But why didn't you tell me?" He threw up his hands. "You knew I was looking for her all this time."

"Because I didn't want you to know," she said emphatically. "Trust me, I did feel guilty because I let on I knew nothing, but you were writing an article and I don't want my name out there. I still don't. I trust you'll keep it a secret." She struggled to get up. "And now I've got to deliver these gifts. There are several sad people out there and I want to give them some cheer, and maybe hope."

He understood her wanting to deliver the baskets and why she had been out in this snowstorm. It was important.

"How about I take you?"

"No, you don't have to do that. It's not far. That's why I was walking."

"I know, but I want to."

"But I don't want to be a burden."

"You're not, Cassie. You could never be."

Silence then, "Okay."

He helped her to his truck, happy to see she actually was able to walk, albeit slowly, and after putting Charlie in the back seat, Cassie directed him to the three places to drop off baskets, all of them houses not far from the bed and breakfast. She made him park down the road. That way no one would hear a car and look out their windows. She wanted, as always, complete anonymity.

"Now, hurry," she said. "Scoot up to those doors and leave the basket outside. Then run."

He did as he was told and enjoyed the mysterious circumstances surrounding the whole rainbow giving. It was shrouded in darkness and beautiful in its delivery. It was all about the giving, wanting nothing in return.

"That was exciting," he said, after dropping off the last basket. "And then you just go home?"

"Well, usually I sit on a bench by the river for a while, stargazing, but the weather's not cooperating tonight."

"Is there one closer to the road, where you don't have to walk too far to get to it?"

"Yes, there is." She clasped his hand. "Would you mind stopping there? And joining me?"

"I'd be honored."

She directed him to a bench only a few steps from where he could park his truck.

He helped her there, then released Charlie, holding tight to his leash. He needn't worry the pup would take off, because he instantly jumped up on the bench to cuddle with Cassie. It was obviously a well-rehearsed routine. Sitting beside her, he enjoyed the star gazing or rather the Cassie gazing. He couldn't seem to take his eyes off her.

Bam. A shooting star burst across the sky.

"That's what I look for," said Cassie. "It reminds me of my mother, and I luckily manage to see one after every gift giving. Like magic."

"It is beautiful," he said. In truth, he was talking about her and thinking about how much he wanted to kiss her. Again.

Should he?

"I sure wish I'd known you were in such pain that day," Cassie said.

"You did," he said putting his hand over hers. "Somehow you were led to me."

"You're probably right."

She looked over and he leaned closer.

Really, should he?

She glanced at him, then looked away.

"Well, we'd better go. Christmas morning will be here soon," Cassie said, starting to stand.

The moment passed. Suddenly, she seemed eager to go. Had she sensed he wanted more?

Too late now.

After driving her home, he helped her in. He got to meet Panda the cat, who stopped for a brief pat on the head, then sashayed by him, swishing her tail, and he laughed when Charlie ran over as if she were his long-lost buddy.

"Charlie loves Panda." Cassie chuckled. "Not sure it's returned."

Jake watched Panda stand still while Charlie licked her ears. "Oh, I think it is," he said.

"Yeah, you're probably right." Cassie opened a door labelled 'Sacred Place.'

"Here. I'd like to show you something."

Jake followed her into the room where there was a desk, filing cabinet, and a very large cupboard. She pointed to a frame on the wall.

"There's the story my grandmother wrote."

"And you don't mind me reading it?"

"No. Go ahead."

It was touching. There, Cassie's grandmother explained the reasons for her anonymous giving. She summed up exactly how he had felt about being the recipient of the rainbow campaign.

"This is truly moving," he said. "Could I use it in a story at some point? I think people need to hear this."

"Sure. No one else has seen it but you. They wouldn't be able to trace it back to me, and you promised to keep my name out of it. Yeah, go ahead."

He quickly snapped a photo of it, and she led him back out to the foyer.

"You sure you'll be okay on your own tonight?" he asked.

"I am. My ankle feels much better."

"Promise to call if you need help?"

"I promise."

After driving back, hating to leave her alone, once again Jake found himself sitting by the window.

He would never forget the feeling of peace and contentment he had felt when helping Cassie rainbow people.

Once upon a time, he had been one of the recipients. He knew firsthand the difference it could make in someone's life.

She had opened up a whole new world to him.

One he liked even better, now that he knew the truth.

He found himself praying for those who received tonight's basket.

May they find hope, he thought.

Like he had.

He crossed his fingers for luck.

Twenty-two

"Was I right to trust Jake, Charlie?"

After all, he was a reporter in town to write a story about the rainbow giver. Me, in fact.

He was the enemy.

I threw my arm around my dog and pulled him tighter against me as he happily licked my face.

"And what do you think, Panda?" My cat was already on my pillow, purring away. One eye opened, then shut.

I loved how contented they both appeared and hoped the tail wags and purring meant I was right.

We were all curled up in my bed and I was trying to sleep.

I really didn't think that was going to happen anytime soon.

I was still wired from the events of the day.

To be honest, I was surprised I had poured my heart out to Jake, telling him all about my mother and grandmother and rainbowing. Why, I even shared my granny's own words and gave him permission to use them.

Most unusual.

Why did I do that?

I was great at keeping a secret.

Then again, I knew why.

I had always viewed Jake as my best friend. My BFF—best friend forever.

As a kid he was my everything.

Then he was gone.

And I don't think I had ever been the same since.

I still couldn't believe Jake had been in that camper truck all those years ago.

To think he was sad and depressed and yet close, and I didn't even know.

I also couldn't get over that moment in the restaurant when he had rolled up his sleeve and showed me the bracelet I had made. It was seared into my brain. And to think he wore it all the time. I had struggled to keep focused, to not let him know it was me who was his mysterious lady, by keeping my face expressionless and my eyes down. I had hoped to reveal nothing. Especially my shock.

I wished I'd known.

I'd have pounded on that truck door until he opened it, and done everything I could to help him.

Panda meowed and stretched, and Charlie laid his head next to hers. Their love for each other resembled what I had always felt for Jake.

Back then, and yes, who was I trying to kid, right now too?

Connecting with him again had been the best thing ever.

He was still the amazing person I remembered.

"Thanks, Mom." I stared at a photo I had of the two of us on my dresser. "Thanks for leading me to him years ago."

I credited her with everything.

And I was sure it was her guidance that urged me on to put those baskets on his truck.

Jake said I saved his life.

I didn't.

I was only a catalyst to shroud him with love so he could stand on his own two feet again.

Usually, I never heard anything back after helping someone anonymously. Just maybe the odd statement about being rainbowed, but that was it.

Which was exactly the way I wanted it.

I just hoped to help in some small way.

To realize I'd had such an effect on someone, and Jake, of all people, blew me away.

Goes to show you how we never know how we can touch someone.

I also couldn't believe I'd slipped, fallen, and Jake was the one to find me. Then again, the bed and breakfast was the only house in Rainbow that faced the river, and he happened to look out at that moment.

My mom's wish?

Probably.

And of course, the fact I was carrying rainbow baskets was a dead giveaway, making him guess correctly that I was the rainbow giver.

But you know, it felt good sharing my secret with a friend.

Still, I never wanted my identity out to the public.

The whole focus was to help people anonymously and I didn't want anyone to interfere with that concept.

Ever.

I didn't have to worry though, because even in the midst of my doubts, I really did trust Jake to keep it secret.

After all, he had promised.

And ... pinky-sweared.

It was all going to be okay.

Twenty-three

What was that?

Drowsy, not quite awake, Cassie's eyes popped open.

Panda, who was sharing her pillow, didn't move, not even an eye roll.

Obviously, nothing shook her sweet cat.

Had she heard something?

Was that what woke her?

Something poked the back of her head.

Snuggled under the covers, Cassie pulled them off her face, turned around slowly and laughed out loud as Charlie jumped on her, smothering her with kisses, tail wagging so fast it swished against the sheets. Fortunately, she had a long pillow, and Panda wasn't disturbed. How wonderful to wake up to this. Charlie's kisses and Panda's purring. She was in heaven.

"Merry Christmas, sweetie." She pulled him into a hug, loving how happy he was to see her. "Is it time to get up?" He barked his approval.

Panda kept on sleeping, obviously not ready to greet the day.

Then Cassie remembered.

Christmas was here.

And it promised to be a great one. First, her parents were home and not only were Jill and Don joining them but also Jake.

Jake.

Her eyes glazed over as memories of the night before swooped in to greet her. It had been such fun delivering the gift baskets with him. It was just the way it was when they were kids – the laughter, joking, teasing. He always had the ability to make even the smallest task enjoyable.

But...when they were sitting on that bench, she almost leaned over and kissed him. Thank goodness she had stopped herself and left fast.

Don't think about that. Remember...Jake would be leaving Rainbow soon. And besides, she had no idea if he would have even wanted to kiss her.

Wow.

She still couldn't believe she had shared with him the rainbow legend and her gramma's words.

Now, that was trust.

At least if he used it in an article, no one would trace it back to her, since no one else had seen it. Besides, the article would be in Manitoba, not in the Rainbow paper.

Charlie barked as if to say, *excuse me, have you forgotten about me?*

"Oops, sorry, boy. I need to let you out and then go over my list of what to do again."

Wiggling her ankle, she realized it felt much better and when she glanced down; it didn't look swollen at all. Thank goodness she had listened to Jake and used that ice pack. Slowly easing out of bed, also trying not to disturb Panda, who was now stretched across all of her pillow, she tested to see if she could put weight on it. Yes, she could. Good. She'd have to be careful in case it was still tender, but for the most part staying off it and resting, seemed to have worked wonders.

Trying not to put too much pressure on her ankle, she pulled her winter parka over her pajamas, grabbed her flashlight, and led Charlie out of her apartment, down the hall, and out the back door to a place behind the building. It was a large grassy area, of course, covered in snow at the moment. Since it was still dark and while Charlie took care of business, Cassie looked up, always amazed at the twinkling stars lighting up the sky. Crossing her fingers, she stared, hoping to see a shooting star, and sure enough she got her wish as one shot out, leaving a trail of even brighter light. She always managed to see one when she really needed it. Luck? Maybe. Wishful thinking? Could be. Although she liked to think it was a sign from her mother – that she was always nearby watching over her.

"Hey, Mom, I'm always thinking of you at Christmas. Sure wish you were here. Oh, and I hope it was okay I told Jake. I know you always liked him."

Hearing her voice, Charlie scampered to her and, blowing a kiss to the heavens, she led him back to the apartment and to the kitchen, relieved her ankle still seemed okay.

"Here's your food, sweetie." Placing his bowl down beside his water dish, Cassie quickly brewed coffee and toasted bread.

While waiting for it to be done, she took a slow walk around her living room, making sure everything looked ready. She hit a switch by the door and her tree burst into blue, red, and green twinkly lights and her train started up, circling it, and sending off exciting vibes into the air with its occasional horn blowing. She eyed her Christmas elf knickknacks perched on a shelf along one wall, and her collection of snow globes displayed across the mantle of her fireplace. Everything clicked together, creating a festive look to the whole room. She was happy with it.

Next, she entered the dining area where a bright red tablecloth covered the massive oak table she had discovered at an antique auction. In the middle stood a large glass angel, given to her by her class. Running her hand over it, she was happy to see rainbow colors reflected in its glassy interior, recalling how their gift brought tears to her eyes at their thoughtfulness.

"This way you'll know your wonderful mom will always be with you," Jarod Smythe, the student representative, had said. "She's your special angel."

One day she had brought in cookies to share, and they had asked if she still baked with her mom. She explained her mother had passed away when she was a teenager. They had expressed surprise that she had lost a parent when she was young, not much older than them. Hence the beautiful, thoughtful gift, which was the perfect centerpiece.

Reassured that everything looked just fine, she felt she was ready.

Settling down at the kitchen table with coffee and now cold toast, still tasty with heaps of jam on it, she ran down her list of things to do. Her main job was the turkey and she needed to get it in the oven soon. Better get on it right away since they were eating in the afternoon, as per tradition. Shoving the last piece of toast in her mouth, she got to work getting it ready. After stuffing it and basting it, she carefully placed it in the oven, setting the timer. She'd never cooked one, and admittedly was nervous. The dinners she provided in her baskets were from cooked turkeys she'd purchased in a nearby town, because she didn't trust she could bake one properly. But for Christmas, she wanted to cook her own, making her dad proud.

"I'd better call him, though, right Charlie? To make sure I didn't leave out a step?" He barked his approval. All right, yes, she talked to her dog and cat as if they were human, but she was also sure they understood. "After all, Dad was the turkey cooker as I grew up. Now where is my purse with my phone? Oh, good morning, Panda." She giggled as her cat wandered into the kitchen meowing in response to her greeting. She was probably really saying, "Okay, where's my food?" Cassie placed her bowl down, grateful Charlie had finally figured out that was hers, not his, although he eyed it hungrily.

"Now, where is my purse?"

She also wanted to remind her dad to bring the mashed potatoes. "No one makes them like me," he always boasted. But he seemed to be busier after he retired and she wanted to make sure he wouldn't forget, especially since he'd just arrived home.

But just where was it?

Usually, she left it on a chair by the door.

Nope, it wasn't there. She walked through each room while Charlie attempted to sniff it out and even checked under the bed.

No purse. No phone.

Had she left it in her car?

"Back in a minute, you two."

She threw her coat on and went out to check. Looking on the seats and under them, even in the trunk, she came up with nothing. It simply wasn't there.

She must have left it at Jake's. It had been in the bag with the baskets, but she had taken it out in his room to check the time. Guess she'd forgotten to put it back. But she had no phone to call him and she needed it now. Besides her phone, she had a necklace in her purse she had to wrap for her stepmother.

Going back inside, she picked up her dog's leash. "C'mon, Charlie. Let's go get it. We'll be back soon, Panda."

She drove over to the bed and breakfast and noticed Jake's truck wasn't there.

"You stay here, sweetie. I'll just be a few minutes."

She hurried in.

"Hi there."

Holly looked up from her desk. "Oh, hi Cassie. How can I help you?"

"Well, I visited Jake last night and accidentally left my purse there."

"Sorry. He's not here. He left about half an hour ago. Something about a meeting he had set up."

A meeting? On Christmas Day?

"Do you think you could let me in? For a second?" She explained about her phone.

"Sure. That's not a problem." She handed over the key. "We can't do without our phones, that's a given."

"I agree. My whole schedule is on it." Cassie started to rush, then reminded herself to walk slowly to not set off her ankle. Opening the door, she looked around and spotted her purse on the floor under the chair she'd been sitting on. Not easy to see and Jake had probably missed it. Good. She picked it up, but as she turned to leave, a headline from his laptop jumped out at her.

Rainbowed, by Jake Williams

Her heart skipped a beat.

Twenty-four

Was he still writing an article on this?

On her?

Jake promised he wouldn't.

He had asked to use her granny's words about anonymous giving, and she didn't mind that, but she didn't think he'd be talking about rainbowing. That brought it closer to home. That could out her.

Stop it, Cassie. You're being nosy.

But she just couldn't resist. She was in self-preservation mode, taking into account she'd been vulnerable before him and had told him a whole lot.

She leaned over his desk.

Scanning the article quickly, she read about Jake hitting rock bottom and how an anonymous giver had saved him.

And guess what! I found my mysterious giver, Jake wrote. *And it was a surprise. I'm sure my readers will be shocked when you hear her name. It turns out the rainbow giver is...*

It ended there. Or more likely he got interrupted before he could finish it.

Cassie felt sick. Like someone had kicked her in the gut.

No way.

He was going to name her?

Betray her?

But he promised.

The phone rang, startling her, and words spilled out into the quiet. *Hey Jake, your cell must be turned off. Hope you have your article ready with the big reveal. I'm looking forward to it, but I do need it soon. Sounds like you've made huge progress. Can't wait to read it.*

That must be his brother.

He'd made progress? He'd done more than that. Jake knew the truth. Had he told his brother? Did the desire for a scoop outweigh his promise to her?

Sure looked like it.

Panic set in.

Breathe, Cassie, breathe.

She had to get out of there.

Picking up her purse, she hurried out of the room, leaving the key at the desk.

"See you," Holly said, coming out a side door. "Merry Christmas."

"Oh, yes, Merry Christmas, Holly. Thanks for letting me get my purse."

She held it up.

"No problem."

Rushing out the door, she got in the car fast, and took off. Charlie barked his greeting, and she could barely acknowledge him.

She was so angry, tears flowed.

Jake had let her down. Again.

They'd even pinky-sweared.

How dare he? He'd hurt her as a kid and now as an adult. She never should have trusted him.

Should she call him and tell him not to come for Christmas dinner?

But then she pictured him alone on Christmas Day, just like that Christmas years ago.

No, she couldn't bring herself to do that to him.

Should she talk to him about what she had seen?

No, he'd just lie. Or make a false promise again.

Was she over-reacting?

No. She saw where he was going to add her name, and besides, his brother said he was waiting for the big reveal. Obviously, something Jake said must have led him to believe that.

She'd just have to endure today, try to put on a happy face and not ruin Christmas for her guests, and after he left, never speak to him again. It was over. For the second time.

Arriving home, she took Charlie for another potty break, then opened the door to her apartment to find her dad and mom already there. A much-welcomed sight for her and her dog, for Charlie was beside himself with two of his favorite people he hadn't seen in a while.

"Hope you don't mind," Adrian said. "You weren't here, so we just let ourselves in."

"Oh, no problem at all. That's why I gave you your own key. I'm just happy to see you." She wrapped her arms around her dad, then her mom. "Sounds like you had a wonderful time." She was definitely glad they were there, but in truth wished she'd had a bit more alone time to process Jake's betrayal.

"Yes, it's good to be home," Adrian said. "By the way, I sneaked a peek at your turkey and it looks perfect. Oh, and the potatoes are in the fridge, ready to be heated when it's time."

"Oh, good. Thank you." She couldn't even imagine eating, she felt sick to her stomach.

"Are you okay?" Adrian asked. "You look upset."

Darn. Get it together, girl.

“Oh, I’m fine.” She planted a huge smile on her face, hoping it looked sincere. “Just have some things to do. A few last-minute gifts to wrap. Be right back.”

She hurried into the bedroom, where Panda was still on her pillow, half in and half out of the covers, as if she’d tucked herself in.

“Hey, girl.” She wrapped the cat in her arms seeking her warmth. “How will I handle being around him today?”

Panda reached up and licked her face.

“You think I’ll be okay?”

Another lick.

“Thanks, sweetie.”

Panda’s purring also soothed her, as she gently put her back on her pillow and tucked her back in.

“Do you need some help in there?” her mom yelled. “I love to wrap.”

“No, thanks. I’ll be right out.”

Some people thought it was weird that she called her stepmom ‘mom.’ But it made sense to her. A full year after her mother had passed, her dad met Janice when she moved to Rainbow, and was in his hardware store shopping. She was a widow and they had struck up a friendship over what nails to use to hang a heavy picture in her dining room. He had ended up volunteering to help her and they hit it off. She was an amazing companion to her dad and wonderful to her. So ‘mom’ it was. It just seemed easier and natural.

“You okay, honey?” This time it was her dad.

Smarten up, Cassie. They’d come to visit and here I was hiding in my bedroom.

“Coming right out.”

She quickly wrapped the necklace, a lovely photo of her dad riding a horse that Jill had given her at the fundraiser, and hurried out to put them under the tree just as Jill and Don arrived. She usually wasn’t last minute when it came to wrapping gifts, but she’d been really busy lately.

"We brought champagne." Jill waved the bottle in the air. "To celebrate. You saved the horse farm."

Cassie laughed. "I did not. It was Lainey's idea, and everyone pitched in and helped."

"No, it was you," Don said. "You made it happen."

"Sorry. Can't take credit for it." Cassie smiled but kept glancing towards the door, waiting for Jake. She wasn't looking forward to it, but would have to deal with it somehow. No shouting matches on Christmas Day was a given.

Hearing her timer go off, she hurried to the kitchen to check the turkey. It looked good so she put it back in to keep it warm.

"Merry Christmas."

She knew that voice.

She turned to see Jake stroll in. He looked happy to see her and was carrying a white bakery box with the words the Sanctuary Breakfast Nook stamped on it.

"Hope you don't mind. I walked in and everyone said you were here."

"That's okay," Cassie said. She wanted to scream and yell at him but instead, dropped her head. She couldn't bear to meet his eyes, so she hurried to the counter and fussed with the basket of rolls instead.

He followed her. "How's your ankle?"

"Much better."

"I brought brownies baked by Kelly. She said you love them."

"I do, thanks." She took the box, pulled out a plate, and started placing them on it.

"You sure you're okay?" Jake asked.

She could hear the confusion in his voice. Considering how close they'd been the night before; she was sure it must appear strange to see her not as friendly.

Tough.

He was messing with the rainbow mission, and it just wasn't cool.

"Yes, I'm fine. Um, do you mind taking this to the table?" She literally shoved the basket of buns in his hands.

"Oh, sure." He paused. "But do you want to talk about it? Did something happen? You seem upset."

Could he not just leave her alone? She was back to wanting to scream again.

"Yeah, yeah. I'm okay."

He finally left the kitchen.

Her favorite brownies.

He had outdone himself.

Normally she would have eaten two of them by now, but somehow, they were no longer appealing. Did he bring them to cover for the fact he was nothing but a traitor?

Forget about him. It was Christmas. Focus on that.

Brushing away a tear, Cassie busied herself with the potatoes.

"Can I help?" Jill asked.

"Oh, sure." If Jill were here, at least that would save her from Jake's bothersome questions.

Between the two of them, they got to work preparing and carrying dishes to the table ignoring Jake's offers of help, as well as the others. She told them all to just relax, since they had everything under control. Jill even got her laughing with stories of the horses' antics that morning.

Finally, the turkey.

After calling everyone to the table, Cassie handed the knife to her dad. "Would you do the honors?"

"I would love to." He sliced it like a pro. "Now before we eat, we need to say grace. And it's customary for the newest person to lead us. That means you, Jake. The rest of us know each other fairly well."

Cassie groaned inside. She didn't need to hear from him in the form of a prayer.

"Oh, please don't put him on the spot," she said.

"That's okay. I'd be honored." Jake bowed his head, paused for a second, then said, "Thank you, God, for this wonderful food lovingly prepared, and for everyone here. Thank you for saving the horse farm and also thank you for bringing me back to Rainbow and for helping me reunite with Cassie. Also, please take care of those less fortunate than us on this special day. May each one of them find hope. Amen."

She almost rolled her eyes at the sentiment but got busy passing food back and forth.

They ate and toasted, and the conversation was merry and fun. She even joined in a few times, especially when the topic got around to the horse farm again. This time Don joined Jill and regaled stories of Painter, their border collie, who used to sleep with them in their bed, until she fell in love with Jasper the horse. Now she had to be with Jasper every second and even joined him in the stall every night to snooze. They had become inseparable.

Cassie sensed Jake looking at her from time to time, but she just ignored him. And then her dad got on the topic of telling tales of their time in Prince Edward Island which elicited a lot of laughs as well. Especially when he said they had paid for their campsite, then pitched their tent beside a grouping of tents that turned out to be a television production, not a real camping area. They'd missed the sign that said, 'Do not camp here.' The next morning they'd rolled out of bed to cameras and realized their mistake. Cassie laughed so hard she had tears rolling down her face, picturing her unshaven, disheveled dad exiting the tent with a camera capturing every move.

Finally, supper was over, dishes were done, and they gathered to exchange gifts. Cassie had purchased one for Jake but didn't feel like giving it to him. But considering Jill had helped her with it, she felt she had no choice.

"This is for you, Jake." She handed him a large, gift-wrapped package after most of the presents had already been opened.

"Thank you." She noticed his eyes were warm and twinkling as he smiled at her. "And this is for you." He picked up a gift from under the tree. She hadn't seen him put it there, and had figured the brownies were his gift. This was a surprise.

"Oh, thanks. You first, though," she said.

He slowly pulled the wrapping paper off, so slowly she felt like screaming, 'Hurry up and get it over with,' and stared at the photo she'd had framed. "I know this horse. It's Clyde, right?" He chuckled.

"Right. There's more, though." Cassie pointed to an envelope attached to the back.

He opened it. "Hey, I'm sponsoring Clyde for a year? You did this, Cassie? In my name?"

"Yes, this way you'll receive photos and newsletters about your favorite horse all year."

"Thank you. Best gift ever. Now open yours."

She tore off the wrapping paper fast and slid the cover off the box. There inside was a dog and a cat angel. The rainbow of colors sparkling through the glass stunned her.

"They are beautiful," she said. "Thank you." She held them up so the others could see.

"Lainey helped me pick them out. She said you love angels and these two are from the same artist who created the one your students gave you."

Darn, Jake. Did he have to be this thoughtful?

"This is very kind of you."

Overcome with emotion, she jumped up, grabbed a garbage bag, and started tossing the wrapping paper in it.

"Well, we'd better get going," Jill said. "We have an early start tomorrow. For Don's family, Christmas is always held the day after Christmas Day. Thank you for a beautiful time, Cassie, filled with laughter, great food, and fun."

"Yes," Adrian said. "We're heading out too. Thank you as well."

Of course, Jake was the last to go.

He kept trying to get her talking, but she couldn't do it. She had nothing left to clean, and just kept fussing over Panda and Charlie, showing them their new Christmas toys. Finally, he was quiet.

"Well, I'd better get going then," he said.

Great. He was taking the hint that he wasn't wanted there.

"Okay," she agreed, too quickly, judging by the look on his face.

"You sure you don't want me to help clean up?" he asked. "We left those pots to soak. I don't mind scrubbing them."

"No, thanks. I can do it."

She handed him his coat.

"Cassie, what's going on? You've barely looked at me all day."

"Nothing's wrong."

He walked to the door and looked up.

She did, as well.

Oh, no.

She forgot she'd hung mistletoe there. She should have taken it down.

She backed away.

He moved forward.

Out of the corner of her eyes, she saw him lean in for a kiss.

She stepped back even further.

"No, Jake."

She felt a twinge of guilt watching his eyebrow shoot up.

"Is there something wrong?" he asked.

"No. But it's best we don't see each other again."

"Pardon?"

"Just go."

He walked out the door, turned, started to say something but she was having none of it.

She shut the door in his face.

Bang.

Rude, yes.

But better than standing there crying her eyes out in front of him.

Twenty-five

"I shouldn't have tried to kiss her," Jake thought, as he drove back to the bed and breakfast. "What was I thinking?"

But he did know. He'd been thinking about how wonderful it was to be friends with Cassie again and how peaceful he'd felt delivering those baskets with her. And of course, he'd been caught up in the Christmas spirit of love.

And mistletoe.

But friends?

Really?

Who was he trying to kid?

What he felt was definitely more than just friendship. But she obviously didn't feel the same. She'd barely looked at him all day. Maybe she regretted letting him in on the 'rainbow' campaign secret.

And now he'd ruined everything.

He wished he hadn't noticed that mistletoe, because when he saw it, he seemed to have lost his mind. After all, the thought of kissing her was something he liked. A lot.

Pounding his fist against the wheel, he groaned in frustration. All he could think about was how much he wanted to talk to Cassie more about her rainbow mission. He was fascinated. He also wanted to tell her what he'd been doing that morning and who his appointment was with. He had been hoping to get her alone for a chat, but that hadn't worked out. Not only had she not looked at him, but she'd also avoided him as much as possible. She wasn't even overly thrilled with his Christmas gift, one he was excited about because Lainey helped pick it out at Joyfest. Life truly sucked at the moment.

Arriving back to the bed and breakfast, he was glad he didn't run into Holly since he wasn't in the mood for small talk. He hurried to his room where he texted Cassie several times, still hoping to talk, but once again, no response.

Better get to work.

He still had an article to write.

Sitting at his computer he deleted his previously unfinished one, which was really just a bunch of useless words written before he had discovered Cassie was his mysterious woman. He started fresh with an altogether different angle to his story, writing completely from his heart. Fortunately, it flowed, and he was nearly finished when his phone rang. Pulling it out of his back pocket, he hoped it was Cassie.

It wasn't.

"Hey there, how's the article coming along?" asked Evan.

"Almost done. I'm about to hit send shortly."

"Good. Hate to ask, but is there any chance you could come back early? Two of my reporters are off sick and I'm run ragged trying to get the paper done in time."

"Sure, I can do that." After all, what was the point of staying since his visit had turned into a disaster?

"I hope you didn't spend Christmas alone as usual."

"No, I got invited to someone's place." He could hear the excited giggles of his nephews in the background.

"I'll have to hear all about it when you get back," Evan said.

"I'll tell you everything then, now get back to your kids. Judging from the laughter I hear it sounds like they're having fun."

"They sure are with those video games you gave them. They had to teach me how to play them. Thanks, by the way. You always know exactly what they want."

"Well, they have no problem letting me know," Jake said. "Bailey announced I was his backup in case Santa forgot to bring them. He even gave me a list of items he wanted."

"Really?" Evan broke out into a peal of laughter. Jake was glad to hear him happy for a change. "I'll have to have a talk with those boys not to be greedy."

They chatted for a while, then hung up. Jake put the finishing touches to his article and sent it off, hoping it was okay.

Walking over to the window, he looked out, sad to leave. But he might as well, since Cassie obviously wanted nothing to do with him. Anyhow, his brother needed his help and he wanted to be there for him, just like Evan had been there when he had hit rock bottom. He glanced at his watch. Eight o'clock. Why wait? Might as well head out now.

After throwing clothes in his knapsack, he gathered up his computer and a few bags, and went to the desk to settle his bill.

"You're leaving?" Holly asked.

"Yes. I need to get back to work."

"But I thought you were looking forward to a full two weeks off."

"I was. But things change."

"I'm sorry to hear that."

She looked puzzled and he felt he should share more, feeling she deserved a better answer, but he couldn't bring himself to do that.

"Um, you're not upset that I let Cassie into your room, are you?"

"Pardon?"

"She forgot her purse there. I let her get it."

That was a surprise. He hadn't noticed her purse had been left behind.

"No, I'm not upset over that." He certainly didn't want sweet Holly bothered. She had done a lot to make his stay wonderful.

"Oh, I forgot to give you this earlier." He handed her two gifts. "For you and your mother."

It was nothing much. Just some holiday candles that he had overheard them saying how much they liked them.

"You didn't have to do this, but thank you. Hope to see you again."

"Me, too. You went out of your way to be kind to me and I appreciate that."

"You will always be my hero." Holly grinned. "Here, take some cookies for the road." She placed several in a bag and handed them over.

"Thanks." When he arrived home, he was going to arrange for flowers and a thank-you card to be sent to Holly and her mother. Oh, and something for Kelly too. He was leaving once again without saying goodbye.

He hurried out of the bed and breakfast, got in the truck, and tried Cassie one more time. Nope, she wouldn't answer. Time to get going, but he had one more stop to make and one more favor to ask. He made another quick call, then started the truck.

Pulling out of town, he turned on his radio, singing along to Christmas carols, trying to cheer up and forget about how he'd blown it. Of course, it didn't help that the songs reminded him of singing them with Cassie. He quickly turned to another station with no Christmas music. That was better.

He also tried to remember the directions to his last destination in Rainbow and was relieved when he saw the Joyful Rescue sign. Fortunately, he'd gone the right way. Pulling up to the office, he grabbed a large brown envelope sitting on the passenger seat and headed in. Jill looked up from her computer.

"Jake. Good to see you again. I was surprised you called. I figured you'd still be at Cassie's."

"Well, I have the papers you wanted me to look over." He handed her the envelope.

"Oh, I'm sorry you had to interrupt your Christmas to look at them."

"No problem. Great news. They all look in good order."

"Thank you." She pulled open her purse. "How much do you charge?"

He was startled. "Nothing at all."

"Are you sure?"

"I'm sure."

The door opened and in walked Don with Gladys. With a bark of excitement, she ran right to Jake. He squatted down to pet her. "Hey, girl. How would you like to come home with me?" She licked his face, her tail wagging.

"I think that's a yes," Don said, laughing.

"I'm thrilled you phoned to ask if you could adopt her," Jill added, clapping her hands. "She adores you."

Jake swung the pup up in his arms. "The feeling's mutual."

"Now I've packed her dog bed, toys she loves, and some treats," Don said, pointing to a package and a large bag by the door.

"And this is for you," Jake said, handing him a small white envelope.

"Nope. You're not paying for her," Jill said. "You've given us too much already."

"A deal is a deal." He put the envelope on the desk.

They walked him to his car and helped him load up the dog's gear and secured her in a crate for the drive.

"I'm not being nosy or anything," Jill said. "But are you leaving town? I see your knapsack in the back."

"Yes, I'm going back home."

"Now?" Don asked.

"Yes." He saw them exchange a glance.

"Does Cassie know?" Jill asked.

"I can't get hold of her."

"Oh."

Jake could tell Jill wanted to know more but couldn't bring himself to say anything. "Well, I'd better get going."

"Hope to see you again." Jill hugged him, then Don did as well. "And thank you for all of your help."

"No problem. Thank you for all the great things you do." He got in his truck.

Waving at the two of them watching him drive away, he began his trek out of town.

Goodbye, Rainbow, he thought.

Thank you for reminding me that kindness and compassion reigned supreme in this tiny town.

It was a place filled with love.

He would never, ever forget it.

Twenty-six

The sign heralding the province of Manitoba rose before Jake.

"We're here, Gladys. I can't wait to show you where I work and live."

She barked her approval, which had him laughing. "Looks like we're developing some good communication."

Driving through the night with less traffic on the road, and then all day, it seemed as if it had taken no time at all. He'd made brief stops for gas, food, and potty breaks for Gladys and once he realized his pup could sleep through music, he'd continued to sing along to the radio to keep himself awake. He just wanted to get home fast. He had a lot to do, both with helping his brother get the paper out on time and also with the changes he wanted to make in his life. Good changes, he hoped.

Jake glanced at his watch. It was nine in the evening, and he longed to head off to bed, but first things first. When he arrived at Pullton, the small town he lived in, he drove over to the newspaper office, knowing his brother would be there. He always popped back in the evening to make sure everything was in order.

Pulling into a parking spot, he slowly eased out of the car, stiff from all the driving, stretched, then let Gladys out of her crate. Snapping on her leash, he led her up the stairs and opened the door.

"This is where I work," he announced proudly, unhooking Gladys' leash, giving her time to sniff around.

He then headed to the little kitchen area, his pup following behind, happy to see coffee already made. He poured himself a cup after putting down food and water for Gladys.

"There you go, little girl."

"Who's this?"

He looked over to see Evan walking in, bearing down on him, pulling him into a hug. Jake held on a little tighter, always grateful to have a brother as wonderful as Evan.

Pulling back, he said, "I'd like you to meet Gladys. Gladys, this is Evan."

"Nice to meet you." Evan bent down to pet the pup while Jake sipped his coffee gratefully, needing the caffeine to stay awake. It'd been a long time since he had pulled an all-nighter.

Straightening up, Evan said, "Thanks for sending in your article."

Jake sucked in his breath, waiting for the verdict.

"I love it."

Whoosh. He blew the air out in relief.

"It's not the one I thought I'd receive," continued Evan. "But I have to admit it's touching and just right for our next edition. I like the different angle you took and it gives much food for thought." He winked. "I must say, though, it's the best writing I've ever seen you do. You utterly outshone yourself this time."

It was because he let his heart guide him, Jake thought. But mostly, it was because of Cassie's effect on him.

Don't think about her.

Jake tried to muster up a smile as he walked to his desk and sat. "I'm glad you like it."

"I do. But hey, I know I asked if you could come back sooner, but I never expected you to be here this fast." Evan pulled up a chair and sat across from him. "You must have flown here in that truck of yours."

"I stopped a few times but mostly just kept driving. I wanted to get here to help you and thought I could work on some editing tonight."

"I think you should get some sleep first."

Jake yawned. "You may be right."

Evan leaned forward. "What happened in Rainbow? You didn't sound good on the phone."

"A lot." Jake rubbed his eyes. He felt a paw on his knee and saw that Gladys had finished her food. He pulled her up on his lap, smiling as she licked his face.

"Well, at least your pup makes you smile." Evan laughed. "But my guess is that you discovered your mystery woman, and somehow it didn't go as planned."

Jake leaned back in his chair, stretched out his legs, and wondered how much he should reveal.

"You're right," he finally said. "I did find her, by accident, and it was a disaster."

"I take it she wasn't thrilled with you seeking her out and your gratitude?"

"Not in the least. And I was convinced everyone would love to be thanked. I mean, she really helped me."

"Did she read your final copy?"

"No."

"Are you planning on sending it to her?"

"I don't know. Right now, she won't answer my messages. I really made a mess of things."

"No, I did."

"What?" Jake watched his brother intently. "You did not. I was the one there, destroying everything."

"But I was the one who sent you. I doubt you would have gone back if I didn't practically beg you to."

Jake nodded. "Well, you did want me to go, but it was my decision in the end. I agree, it would have made a great story about meeting the woman who helped me when I was down and out. And all anonymously. The only catch was, she didn't want to be recognized or known."

"Well, I guess we all make mistakes. Especially chasing a story and getting caught up in it we forget about people's feelings at times. I'm sorry I put you in this spot."

"Don't be. I went willingly."

"But at least you got a new roommate." Evan pointed at Gladys curled up in his lap, staring up at Jake. "That pup sure loves you."

Jake smiled. "And it's mutual. She stole my heart the moment I met her."

He yawned again.

"Well, I think you need to go home and get some sleep, but I'd love you to join us for dinner tomorrow night. We have a lot of leftovers needing to be eaten." Evan stood, hands on his hips. "And I won't take no for an answer. Besides, the boys will love to meet Gladys."

Jake smiled. "Well, look at you trying to be fierce. Yes, I'll come." It was his turn to sit up and lean forward. "I also have some serious business to discuss with you. Could you fit me in during the day tomorrow for a meeting?"

"You do? A meeting?"

"Yes."

"You're not leaving the paper, are you?"

"Oh, no. Nothing like that."

"Tell me now."

Jake yawned again. "Nope. Later. I'm way too tired to get into a discussion."

"I'm intrigued, and of course I'll fit you in," Evan said. "I always have time for you."

"Great. I'll head off now. See you tomorrow."

Jake got up, leashed Gladys, and drove home to get some well-needed sleep.

But first things first.

He had a presentation to put the finishing touches to before he met with Evan the next day.

He hoped it would go well.

He also hoped his brother would say 'yes.'

Twenty-seven

"Did you see this article?" Jill stood there, waving a newspaper.

"What article?" Cassie had no idea what she was talking about. Even though school was still out on vacation, she had popped into her classroom every day on the pretense of tidying it up. She had just dusted four times and the room was clean to begin with. Anything to keep busy and try to put Jake's betrayal out of her mind. "Hey, wait a second. How did you know I was here?"

"Because I know you well, and I know you're upset with Jake. I could tell that when you were out riding the other day and you changed the topic every time his name came up." Jill dropped the paper on her desk. "And I know you clean your classroom when you're stressed. And I'm talking about the article Jake wrote. It was re-printed in our paper."

"Not interested." She waited for Jill to ask her about being the 'rainbow' giver since Jake would have revealed her name. She didn't. Cassie always thought she knew or suspected, but said nothing. Now she would have proof. All due to Jake. The rat.

Jill squeezed her shoulder. "Well, at least read the last couple of paragraphs. I'll be in my room for a time doing some paperwork. Come and talk if you need to." She left fast.

Should she read it?

No way.

By revealing her identity, Jake would have destroyed all that her mother and grandmother had stood for. He would have blown her cover.

Nope. She was not reading that article. She was not planning on being hurt by Jake anymore.

The classroom door opened again and in raced Holly.

What was going on?

Why was she here?

And how did everyone know where she was?

"I brought you the..." She waved the town paper. "Oh, I see you have it. Have you read Jake's article?"

"No. And how did you know where to find me?"

"I called your dad. Please, you have to read this. It's a great article about how wonderful our town is."

Cassie shook her head. "Why would you think I would want to read it?"

"Oh c'mon. He was crushed when he left here the other day. I figured you'd feel better about him after reading this."

Did everyone know she was upset with Jake?

"I don't want to have anything to do with that man. He hurt me once, he'll hurt me again."

Holly put her hands on her hips. "How can you really say he hurt you? I see the way he looks at you. It was obvious to me back in school and I wasn't even in your grade. And after all, he took on the biggest bully to save your precious knapsack. Very few would do that and he's still that same kind, wonderful person."

"What are you talking about?"

"Back in elementary when Stuart White grabbed your brand-new pink knapsack and took off with it." She grinned. "You got it back, right?"

"Jake was the one who dropped it off at my front door?"

"Yes. I witnessed the whole thing. I was hanging with my friends in the park when I saw him chasing Stuart. I followed and saw him tackle that bully and get the knapsack back. He also made Stuart promise never to hurt you or anyone ever again." She stamped her foot. "And I saw him put it on your porch and ring the bell."

"But he wasn't there when I opened the door. No one was."

"Yes, he was. He hid in the bushes and watched you. Even I can remember how big your smile was at getting back that knapsack." Holly glanced at her watch. "Oops, I have to go. I must get back to the inn." She hugged Cassie. "Please, just read this."

Stunned, Cassie sat with a bang.

She still had that pink knapsack.

Her mother had given it to her and she could never bring herself to get rid of it. When Stuart had stolen it, she had been devastated.

Jake had saved it for her.

Taken on the local bully.

She never knew that.

Guess the least she could do was read the article. Or at least the last couple of paragraphs. Nah, the whole thing.

Here goes.

Hands shaking, she picked up the paper.

A Merry Christmas Rainbow by Reporter Jake Williams.

Tears rolled down Cassie's face as he outlined in detail what happened to him and how he ended up living in a truck. His words were vivid, making the reader really feel his pain, as if they were right in that truck with him. She felt her heart snap in two. However, the next words made her gasp.

One morning I woke to find someone I didn't know had left me a care package, tied to the mirror outside my truck, to show me I was cared for. Even if it was by a stranger.

Here it was.

Her unveiling.

She guessed Jill and Holly didn't want to say anything until she'd read it herself.

Cassie took a deep breath and exhaled slowly.

Keep going.

Bracing herself, she continued reading through the details, still amazed at the effect her anonymous giving had on him.

Five years later, I went back to the town of Rainbow.

It was coming soon, Cassie thought.

I wanted to thank this person for saving my life. I truly believed I was doing a good thing by seeking out my helper and letting her know I was okay, thriving, all because of her. I wanted to throw her a big party, snap a photo of her, and write a newspaper story about how kind she was. I wanted to give her all the accolades she deserved.

On the way to finding her, without even meeting her yet, I learned a lot about her.

I found out my mystery woman gave from the heart all year round, not just at Christmas. I also discovered that no one would give up her identity. Either they didn't know or kept it a secret out of respect. I believe it was the latter.

I was also having no luck discovering her.

Then, purely by chance, on Christmas Eve—the five-year anniversary of my hitting rock bottom—I discovered who was behind it all.

I met her. Face to face. The woman who saved my life.

And she taught me a lot.

She taught me about something I had never really thought about—anonymous giving and...that not everyone wanted or needed to be thanked.

I also discovered that her anonymous giving was a campaign passed on by her grandmother to her mother and then to her. She even shared the exact words her grandmother had written, given to her by her mother.

Here they are:

"I have always been a giver. I have often been the first person to jump in to help others. Then a day arrived when I needed help, and someone was there for me. Anonymously. At first, I was uncomfortable with this. I wanted to know who did this so I could thank them and pay them back. I never found out who my giver was, but I discovered one thing: I was so focused on finding out who did it that I never enjoyed what they had given me until I stopped looking, and it completely changed my life. I found out that gifting someone anonymously is a pure form of love. It is recognizing that someone is in need and reaching out to them without them knowing. The only thing important is the other person. It is telling them I see you, I hear you, I love you. The giver does not want to be recognized or be thanked. They are simply giving from the heart in all its purity. I also learned that when you receive a gift rooted and bathed in love, even though it is hard, it is important that you open your heart to receive this gift. You don't have to worry about thanking someone or being beholden to them. No strings are attached. Please, allow their thoughtfulness to fill you with strength and courage. Allow it to heal you. This is what anonymous giving is all about. It is love at its best. In its truest sincerity. If you are lucky enough to receive an anonymous gift, hold it close to you. Know that you are loved just for being you. Allow the anonymous gift to fill your heart. It will change you forever. Love, Granny.

Jake continued.

There are many forms of love and caring for one another.

There are random acts of kindness and giving anonymously as well.

But I had never thought of anonymous giving as a mission, a quest, a private campaign. I had never thought of giving quietly and purely on a regular basis.

However, I remember what this act of giving did to me. I can summon up that feeling of recognizing that someone—someone I didn't even know—valued me, not for something I did for them, but simply by just being. Being myself. In fact, she didn't even know me.

My anonymous giver filled my heart with hope and helped me begin the long way back to myself.

Some people may think it's idiotic to constantly give without a thank you coming their way.

Not at all.

It changed my life the first time and once I understood the concept behind it, it changed my life for the second time.

Allowing the love that healed me to flow to someone else's heart anonymously made a huge difference in my life and maybe in someone else's. It made me more aware of others' pain, their needs, their silent cries.

And yes, I have done some anonymous giving lately, but I can't tell you about it, because of course, it's anonymous.

Try it.

I guarantee it will rock your world.

It did mine.

Cassie sat back, embarrassed. And shamed.

He hadn't given her up after all.

In fact, the only mention of Rainbow was in reference to the name of the town.

She had completely misjudged him.

Twenty-eight

She had to make it better.

Now.

Cassie was mad at herself for accusing Jake of doing something he hadn't done. And even though she was usually a huge fan of communication, she'd blown it.

That must have been an old article she'd seen on his computer when looking for her purse. And she had never even told him what was bothering her and given him the opportunity to explain.

She had allowed her fear of getting hurt to take over and smother her.

In fact, she had ruined Christmas for him.

Stop it.

Stop rambling and do something.

Sometimes you just have to take a leap of faith to make things right. This situation required action...and a leap.

Urged on by a deep sense of urgency to right a wrong, she made a quick call, and was surprised how easy it was. But her mom used to say that *often things worked out well when you were on the right path.*

She finally felt she was on that path.

At last.

Rushing into Jill's classroom, she shouted, "Would you mind giving me a ride to the airport?"

Jill smiled. "Sure, where are you going?"

"Manitoba."

"You got it, girl. I figured Jake speaking nicely of our town would win you over."

Jill didn't know the half of it, thought Cassie.

They made a quick trip to Cassie's apartment, where she filled a tote with Charlie's food and gathered together a few clothes. Eyeing her childhood pink knapsack that still held a special place on a hook in her bedroom, she thought why not. She took it down and stuffed it with her clothes.

Panda was curled up, fast asleep on the bed, so Cassie enveloped her in a big hug. "I won't be long, girlie," she whispered.

"And I promise to take good care of Panda," Jill said, entering the room. "Don't you worry."

Cassie wasn't. Panda adored Jill. She still didn't like leaving her, but her little cat would prefer the comfort of home, rather than an airplane ride.

Snapping a leash on Charlie she said, "C'mon, boy. We're going to see Jake." He barked his approval and followed the two of them out as they carried his crate and her knapsack to the car. She knew he would rather be with her on this journey.

"Are you all ready?" Jill asked, helping her load her belongings in the trunk.

"I am."

"Let's get going."

"Do you think I am doing the right thing?" Cassie asked, as they took off to the airport.

"Yes," Jill said. "You've been upset for days. I'm not even completely sure why, but you need to sort things out." She glanced over, then back at the road. "I've never seen you happier than when Jake is around. Of course, Christmas Day wasn't a stellar example, but I guess that's when everything went off course."

"Yeah, I need to have a good, honest talk with him. I was a real jerk on Christmas Day."

"Not a jerk. I don't pretend to know what was happening, but I believe fear was involved."

"You're absolutely right. It was."

Pulling to a stop in the drop-off parking area at the airport, Jill leaned over and hugged Cassie.

"Good luck. I'm rooting for you," she said. "And toss that fear away. Jake's one of the good guys."

"Thanks, and you're right." Cassie got her stuff from the trunk, waved goodbye, led Charlie through the door, and eventually onto the plane. She was lucky. Because Charlie was small enough, she could have him crated at her feet. Thank goodness. It was his first flight and she wanted him relaxed. At least one of them should be.

Staring out the window, she was excited yet worried about how Jake would receive her. After all, she had been awful to him on Christmas Day. She shuddered at how she had slammed the door in his face. Good grief, she owed him a huge apology.

Tears rolled down her cheek.

Cassie had lost him once; she couldn't lose him again.

All the way there, she rehearsed what she was going to say to him. Over and over and over.

Since the flight was only a couple of hours, they arrived in what seemed like minutes.

"We're here, Charlie," she said as the plane landed.

Suddenly she felt ill.

What if Jake refused to speak to her?

After all, she couldn't blame him.

Stop.

Focus.

Get Charlie somewhere for a potty break.

She led him to a small grassy area out the front door of the small airport and put down some water and food. She then persuaded a taxi driver to let her bring Charlie in his car as long as he remained crated.

"Could you please let us off at the newspaper office? *The Manitoba Times*," she asked.

"Sure, lady, no problem."

"Thank you."

She was shocked to see a for sale sign when he pulled up in front of a small grey building. Was the paper closing? Was Jake out of a job?

"Here you are." The driver got out, opened the trunk, and handed her the knapsack while Cassie rushed to let Charlie out of his crate in the back seat.

"Thanks again." She paid the taxi driver and once more looked up at the newspaper office. This was where Jake worked. At least it was decorated nicely, framed with white lights, strands of garland around the windows, and a brightly colored wreath on the door.

Her heart sped up and she felt lightheaded, knowing she'd be seeing Jake shortly. Nerves rippled through her as she faced the same worried questions. Should she have come? Should she turn around and head back to Rainbow? She rarely made rash decisions. Even her father was shocked when she phoned from the airport and told him where she was going.

Stop it.

She was here and was going to finish what she came to do.

"C'mon, Charlie, let's go in before I chicken out. Time to face our friend."

She hurried up the stairs, opened the door slowly and, hearing music, turned right, and walked to a desk with a 'receptionist' nameplate on it.

No one was there.

"May I help you?"

She looked over to see a man walking towards her. He was tall with dark auburn hair and he looked vaguely familiar. She saw him take in her knapsack and Charlie with raised eyebrows.

"Yes, I'm looking for Jake Williams."

"Sorry, he's not here. But who is this?" He bent down to pet Charlie. Aha, a dog lover.

"This is Charlie. You're Evan, aren't you? Jake's older brother."

He straightened up. "And you're Cassie, right? Cassie Blackburn. Jake said he connected with you during his stay. Although I was off at school the year my family lived in Rainbow, I visited and I recall you spending a lot of time with my brother."

"Yes, that's me."

He scratched his head. "Does Jake know you're coming? He never mentioned it to me."

"Ah, no, he doesn't."

"You flew out to see him?"

"Yes. Er...we had a misunderstanding." Did Jake tell Evan she was the rainbow giver? Did he know?

Don't go there.

Stop being paranoid and thinking something that was probably not true, when in actual fact, Jake had never let her down.

"Oh." Evan smiled. "Well, I think he'll be happy to see you, but you need to move fast. He's flying out today."

He'd like to see her? She hung onto those words, really hoping Evan was right. Wait, he was flying somewhere?

"He is?"

"Yes, come on, I'll drive you to his place and he can explain it to you."

"Oh, I can't put you out like that. If you give me his address, I'll call a cab."

Evan shook his head. "It'd be my honor to give you a lift. Hang on, let me get my coat." He hurried to a door down the hall, opened it, and went in.

Jake was flying somewhere?

Where?

On another story? A new job?

Evan came back fast, picked up the crate and led her to a parking lot out back. She wondered if he had phoned Jake and warned him.

"Is Charlie okay on my lap? Or would you like him crated?"

"On your lap is fine. I'll put the crate in the trunk."

"Did you read his Christmas article?" Evan asked, starting the car.

"Sure did. It was beautiful."

"Yeah, he's a great writer and sure loves Rainbow. I did too, the few times I visited." He pulled up to a small apartment building. "Well, here we are."

"That didn't take long."

"It's actually within walking distance, but with a crate and luggage and snowy sidewalks, I figured I could get you here faster." He got out, hauling the crate out of the trunk for her.

"Are you coming in?" Cassie asked, getting out as well and making sure Charlie was taken care of.

"No. But I am scheduled to take Jake to the airport later." He led her up the steps. "But here, I have a key to the main door. I'll let you in. That way it'll be a complete surprise."

He hadn't told him.

"Thanks, Evan."

"No problem. He's on the second floor. Number two hundred. Oh, and by the way, Jake doesn't know I sent his article to the Rainbow paper."

"No?" Cassie was surprised.

Evan smiled. "No. I wanted your town to read the beautiful things he said about it."

"Thank you. I'm glad you sent it."

"Me, too. Oh, and don't worry. He really will be happy to see you."

"Thanks." Guess she was pretty transparent when it came to her worries.

He turned and walked back to his car.

She was alone. With Charlie, of course, who was staring at her, wondering what to do next.

"Come on, sweetie."

She opened the doors to the stairwell and started walking. Slowly, nervously, in fact, terrified.

Once again, she thought, was this the right thing to do?

Guess she'd know in a few minutes.

When she opened the door to the second floor, an elderly woman was standing in her doorway, holding a box.

"Oh, hello dear. I found this outside my door. Did you put it there?" she asked.

"No, sorry. Wasn't me. Is it something good?"

The lady smiled. "Yes, it's cookies. And my favorite, chocolate chip."

"Well, enjoy."

I bet I know who did it, Cassie thought. Jake—anonymously.

Walking down the hall, she eyed the numbers on the doors.

Number two hundred.

Here it is.

Taking a deep breath and pushing it out slowly, she knocked. Frightened, she almost turned and ran when suddenly it swung open.

Jake stood there, his eyes grew big, and his mouth dropped.

"Cassie? Charlie?" He took a step back. "What are you doing here?"

She stared at him. Hair tousled, red plaid shirt, jeans, bare feet. He was familiar to her, like a warm blanket you could wrap around you, keeping you safe. Her best friend. Someone who she almost let go, again. She hoped this time she wouldn't blow it, especially since all she wanted to do was run into his arms.

"I read your article and I'm sorry I misjudged you." She figured she'd tell him exactly why she was here. No more game playing.

Just then, a bark of joy rang out and a tiny pup squeezed around Jake's legs and covered Charlie with kisses.

What?

"Gladys? Is that Gladys?" Cassie could feel a huge grin stretch across her face as the two pups licked each other's faces, obviously adoring each other.

"I adopted her. I fell in love with this little lady. C'mon in." He backed away from the door so she could enter, followed by the two dogs, while he picked up the crate and moved it indoors.

"Would you like a coffee?"

"Sure." She was amazed Jill had never told her Jake had adopted Gladys.

He led her to the kitchen and while the two dogs played, she sat at the table. "This is a nice apartment, by the way." She had noticed his living room looked cozy and warm, with numerous plants and brown leather furniture atop a multicolored rug. "And I love that your kitchen is painted yellow and is bright and airy."

"I can't take credit for anything, really. I rented it furnished." He handed her a coffee. "Sorry it's not a latte."

"That's okay."

He sat across from her, holding his own coffee. "How did you get hold of my article? It's not online yet."

"Evan had it printed in the Rainbow paper."

"He did? I had no idea."

"I know." She paused. "You didn't give me away."

"No, I wouldn't do that, Cassie. I understand what you are trying to do and I respect you. Talk about changing the world one kind gesture at a time." Pausing, he took a sip. "I bow down to your good work."

"Remember." She smiled. "I don't want thanks, but I saw another article on your computer when I went to get my purse. Obviously, it was an old one. Sorry—I should have told you. I thought you were revealing my name."

"Oh, that explains things. Holly told me you were there, and I should have clued in. It was an old copy I was temporarily writing as I searched for the 'rainbow' giver. I know I pinky-sweared, but I considered talking to you about how I needed to deliver the name for my brother. I owe him a lot. But once I discovered it was you, no way would I tell."

"Thank you."

"No, thank you. You truly saved my life all those years ago." He smiled. "I also have some good news to share. My email has been flooded with people talking about anonymous giving. Many are sharing how it affected them, while others are looking around, becoming more aware of friends, neighbors and family, and wondering how to help them. All anonymously. And Evan wants me to write a follow-up column. Look what you started."

Embarrassed, Cassie felt her face redden. "Actually, it's what my grandmother started." She looked over at the packed bags near the door.

"By the way, where are you going?"

He laughed. One of those big guffaws that she loved.

"I'm flying to Rainbow. I came home because I had a few things to discuss with my brother, plus to help him get that important edition out. Today I was going back to talk to you. A few more hours and you would have missed me here." He kept on grinning. "I was going to stand outside your door until you told me what was bothering you."

"You're kidding, right?"

"No, and another thing. I'm moving back there. My brother and I bought the Rainbow newspaper. I was trying to tell you that might be a possibility on Christmas Day. Evan will do that,

I'll help him a little, but I will open a law practice there as well. James is going to stay on to assist with the transition and continue to write articles."

"Really? You're moving to Rainbow? And you're going back into law?" She grinned back. "That was why you were hanging around on Christmas Day. You were trying to tell me your news?"

"Yes, to both questions. Possible news because I hadn't discussed it yet with my brother." He smiled. "There is a teacher there whom I want to spend more time with."

Yes, definitely a fully fledged blush now.

"And your brother agreed to this?"

"He always loved it there and he and his family are ready for something new."

Overcome with emotion, she stood and did what she had wanted to do from the moment he opened his door. She reached out her arms to hug him. As if anticipating her move, he stood as well, and pulled her into his embrace.

"I also found out you were the one who got my pink bag back, right?" she whispered.

"Yes. Holly must have ratted me out."

"She did." Cassie laughed.

"And you were the one who fed me at school by pretending you didn't want your lunch, right?"

She nodded. "Guess we both helped each other."

"Yes. And this time, we won't rely on trees to communicate. No more mix-ups," he said. "Pinky-swear."

"Pinky-swear." They clasped their fingers together. "Oh, I forgot something." Cassie pushed away and ran to her knapsack. She pulled something out and held it up.

"Mistletoe." He laughed.

"I figure we should start over," she said. "Let's get it right this time."

With one hand holding up the mistletoe, her other hand cupped his face.

He leaned down for a kiss, cut short by two sets of barks.

Laughing, they looked down to find Charlie and Gladys with their paws up on their knees.

“Over here,” Jake said, leading her to the couch.

And there they sat, arms around each other, pups sitting on their laps.

“Here’s to a lifetime of ‘rainbowing’ people,” Jake said.

“You got it,” Cassie said, leaning in for another kiss.

And she was sure, if it was night out, she’d see a shooting star.

Meet Suzanne M. Hurley

Happiness to this author is being curled up with her laptop creating imaginary worlds that flow from her heart. Writing is her passion and dreaming up story lines is her love.

Suzanne was born in Peterborough, Ontario and currently resides in Caledonia, Haldimand County, where on morning walks, she tries out her new plots on the cows, sheep, and numerous wild animals she greets along the way.

Other Works from the Pen of Suzanne M. Hurley

Samantha Barclay Mystery Series:

Changeable Facades - A murder has been committed! No one believes it but a young boy and his high school counselor. Will they catch the killers before he or she strikes again?

Delusions - Narcotics are sweeping Milton High! A student is dead! Lies and Deceit take over, as high school counselor Samantha Barclay is immersed in yet another deadly drama.

Chances – FBI Agent Ryan Leam's son is missing. Psychologist Samantha Barclay risks her life to go undercover at Sacred Heart Academy, seeking truth. The results are shocking and unbelievable.

Shades of Envy – Dead bodies are stacking up! Teenagers want to be vampires! The sheriff is acting secretively!

Psychologist Samantha Barclay sets out on a wild ride to uncover the truth. Her discoveries lead to confrontations of the deadly kind. Will she survive with her life, as well as her heart intact?

Who did it? – Who killed the beloved principal of St. Michael's High School? Newly minted FBI agent Samantha Barclay's first case is to find the murderer. Only one problem. Everyone she meets has a reason to see him dead. Will she uncover who did it – before he or she strikes again?

Love? – Samantha Barclay discovers what people will do in the name of love, when a dead body is discovered in her basement and her beloved step-mother is arrested for murder.

Guilt – Who killed Doctor Ingrid Sayers? High school teacher David Harris says he did. Samantha Barclay disagrees and races against all odds to find the real murderer

The Cookie Club – One by one, the residents of Landon, West Virginia, are dropping dead. FBI/school psychologist Samantha Barclay, sets out to find the killer, before it becomes a ghost town.

Women's Fiction:

Nice Girls Can Win – Lawyer Jessie White is fired, evicted and jilted, all on the same day. Hitting rock bottom, she moves back home and immediately ends up in a sparring match with 'Red', the hunky guy next door. She soon discovers that miracles really do happen and how love often finds you, just when you're not looking.

Wings of the Past – Zoey Avery thinks she is happy, until wedding thoughts infiltrate her marriage-phobic mind. Only one problem – the groom she is dreaming about is a man she hasn't seen in thirteen years.

The Dream Smasher – Best-selling author Tracy Hazel is devastated to discover she is the victim of identify theft, when someone submits a horrid book, claiming she wrote it.

The Christmas Rose – Sparks fly, when Principal Olivia Lyons tries to uncover which student stole a million-dollar Christmas ornament. Her new guidance head thinks she did it. Will she end up in jail, love, or both?

Love Always – Jenna Evans has no idea she is in a coma. She believes she has somehow landed in a fantasy world where everyone is supportive and lives in peace. Will she return to her husband and children? It all comes down to love - real love. What will she choose?

Heart Gifts – Serena's Christmas pageant is the key to saving her mother's bakery. Will she be able to convince archenemy Matt to help before it's too late?

Words of Love – Journalist Ellie O'Brien wants to use her words for good. Is this attainable when often readers believe gossip is the truth? Time will tell.

Young Adult

The Teddy Bear Eye Club – Depressed, fourteen-year-old Mayah Lewis hides from the world, until she befriends new girl, beautiful bald-headed Celeste Daniels. Everything begins looking up, until one day, Celeste disappears.

Dear reader,

I hope you've enjoyed reading this story of the power of anonymous love.

Your opinion is valuable to other readers like you, who may be looking for books like mine.

Please consider taking a few minutes to post a review, however brief, on the site where you purchased this book or on the Wings ePress web page.

You may also want to visit my author page at the Wings' website, where you can find all the other books in my series.

Thank you!

Suzanne M. Hurley

Visit Our Website

For The Full Inventory
Of Quality Books:

Wings ePress, Inc

Quality trade paperbacks and downloads
in multiple formats,
in genres ranging from light romantic comedy to general fiction and horror.
Wings has something for every reader's taste.
Visit the website, then bookmark it.
We add new titles each month!

Wings ePress, Inc.
3000 N. Rock Road
Newton, KS 67114

www.ingramcontent.com/pod-product-compliance
Lightning Source LLC
Chambersburg PA
CBHW060327260626
47160CB00007B/2712

* 9 7 8 1 6 1 3 0 9 8 9 7 4 *